Pretty Lips That Thugs Love 3

By Twyla T.

Copyright

Publishers Note

Published by Cole Hart Presents
This is a work of fiction. Names, characters, places, and events are strictly the product of the author or used fictitiously. Any similarities between actual persons, living or dead, events, settings, or locations are entirely coincidental.

To Join Our Mailing List and Stay Up To Date With New Releases, Sign Up Below!

http://goo.gl/ZQP5K6

Dedication

This book is dedicated to my big brother, Cornelius Jejuan Turner. I can literally write a whole book about this guy and how big his heart is, but I won't. I'll just keep it simple. If there is ever anything that I need, I know that he will make a way. We lost our dad at an early age, and although he can never take his place, that doesn't stop him from doing everything he can possibly can to take up the slack. Every time I have a book to come out, he buys it, reads the dedications and says, "I'm waiting on my shout out but I know you do stuff on your own time,"

You're right brother, and this one is for you! You told me to keep slanging those books because I do it so easy. It's not easy, but I'm definitely gonna keep moving forward. Thank you so much for all of your love and ongoing support. I love you!!

Acknowledgements

As always, I must acknowledge and thank God because without him, none of this would be possible. The ability to sit down and create enjoyable stories is so amazing. People often ask me, how you come up with all of that stuff. The answer that comes out is, I don't even know. It just comes to me, but I had to catch myself recently and start saying, God because it's all him.

Shout out to Cole for keeping the covers and titles hot and always steering me in the right direction.

To every member of Twyla T's Reading Group and Cole Hart Signature Readers Club, Salute to you guys. Y'all are the real MVP's. I can always count on y'all to give it to me straight, no chaser and y'all know that's how I want it. It's very enjoyable to kick back, laugh, and have a good time with y'all. If you haven't checked out the Queens of Urban Fiction Anthology by Cole Hart Presents, go download that now so that you can see which hot stories are available and add them to your kindles.

As always, I put my all into it and I would love to have your honest feedback to help me excel in my passion. When you are done, please leave me a review on Amazon, Good Reads, and/or any of my social media pages so that I can read your feedback and make adjustments. My Facebook, Instagram, and Twitter handles are all @authortwylat

You may also email me at authortwylat@gmail.com

Search Twyla T's Reading Group on Facebook if you love my work and become a supporter! We love to kick back and have fun in there, and there also random giveaways!

Other great reads by Author Twyla T:
We Both Can't Be Bae 1-3
I'll Never Love A Dope Boy Again 1 & 2
My Shawty 1-3 (An Original Love Story)
Pretty Lips That Thugs Love 1-2

Previously in Pretty Lips That Thugs Love 2…

That young nigga Buck had disappeared ever since he tried to rob the trap. Slick and Dub had been looking high and low, but always came up empty handed. What was worse, they found out that he had been skimming off of the top from the other spots, and the one in Black Jack had been his last hit. The one that should have been the biggest, but his ass got punked. Money was still flowing, Slick had found the lawyer to take Tay's case, and him and Amanda were closer than ever before, so shit was good with Slick.

Slick's phone rang as he was about to grab something to eat from Zaxby's. He saw it was one of the workers, so he answered right away. All he needed to hear were the words Buck and Crawford to make him drop what he was doing and leave. He knew those sweet and spicy teriyaki wings was about to hit the spot, but they would just have to wait until another time because business always came first. Amanda was coming to his house for the first time later that evening, but with the call he had just received, he knew that he needed to handle that shit first and he hoped that he would be done before she arrived. Buck lived out in Crawford, but he hadn't been spotted at his house in months. Slick didn't know if he would still be there when he made it or not, but he was headed to light that bitch up.

While he was on the way, he called Dub and told him what the deal was and he knew that they would probably end up out there at the same time. Neither of them gave a fuck that it was barely noon, they had shit that was long overdue that needed to be dealt with. Twenty minutes later, Slick called Dub as he was passing by the old East Oktibbeha County High School. He briefly thought about how they had let the school down and it was such a shame. Dub picked up and when Slick asked him where he was, he told him that he was on Crigler Road which was less than a minute away. They met up at an old abandoned house that was a half of a mile down the road to the right. The house was ducked off behind some trees and not very noticeable unless you were looking for it. Dub wasted no time hopping out of his car and jumping in Slick's black Suburban.

"So what's the plan?" Dub wasted no time asking as he pulled both of his guns out and checked them for ammo.

"I say we bring the punk ass nigga to us. We bout to light up his shit right now and hope that we get him, but if we don't, we know he gonna retaliate. As soon as he come looking, we smoke his dusty ass," Slick firmly stated.

"Sound like a muthafuckin' plan to me, but I want this lil nigga dead now. Long as he done lived after the shit he pulled probably got other muthafuckas thinking 'bout trying us," Dub replied.

"Let's roll," Slick retorted and headed out.

Slick made his way down the road while Young Jeezy blasted through the speakers. Buck lived all the way down the road on the left, and luckily for them, there was a big ass gap in the houses. No one was expecting a drive by in the middle of the day. Right before Slick approached the house, he pulled over to the side of the road because he had a change of heart. He got out and went to the back and pulled out something that he had been having for a long ass time, but never used. He had no idea if it was even going to work, but he was about to test the shit out and see.

"Is that one of them combat laser weapons?" Dub asked with a sly grin on his face when Slick hopped onto the back seat.

"Hell yeah… I didn't know when I was gon' test this shit out, but ain't no better time than now," Slick replied.
He had an old friend in the military that was always able to take and also make some of the newest shit. The last time he was home, he had given Slick a new little toy and told him that it would blow up some shit instantly and kills whoever was inside, whether it be by fire or smoke inhalation, there was no chance of survival.

"I take it I'm driving this bitch," Dub said and hopped over into the driver seat.

"Yep, now let's get it," Slick replied with the weapon aimed and ready.

When Dub approached Buck's house, Slick rolled down the window. He pointed the laser out of the window and when Dub was right in front and slowed down, Slick fired. The house blew up in flames instantly, and Dub sped away before anyone came down the road. On one hand they were glad it was a road that didn't get much traffic, but on the other hand they really didn't give a fuck. Dub drove the long way around before he returned to his car. Before he got out, Slick told him to pick him up at the court on the West Side because he was going to park his truck there and leave it since a basketball tournament was going to be happening that evening.

Three hours later, Slick finally walked through his door after having Dub pick him up and swing him through Hardee's drive thru to grab a burger. He knew Amanda was on her way and more than likely they would eat later, but he was starving and needed to put something on his stomach ASAP. Slick had texted Amanda his address early that morning, so he was expecting her at any minute since she never specified a time. As soon as Slick took a couple of bites from his burger, the doorbell rang. He got up from the couch and opened the door and the smile Amanda wore must have been contagious because he found himself smiling back.

"Hey baby!" Amanda stated excitedly and dropped her overnight bag and hugged Slick.

"I kinda figured you was gonna pop up soon," Slick replied and gave Amanda a kiss.

"Dannggg… you eating already? Where's mine?" Amanda jokingly inquired.

"We can still eat later, but I had to get something to hold me over. I was starving," Slick said as he made his way back over to the couch and sat down. He sighed and took another bite of his burger.

"You must be tired?" Manda asked.

"I really am… it's been a long and stressful day," Slick retorted.

"Well I can make you feel better," Manda told him and moved down and unbuckled his pants.
Amanda released his dick from his pants and boxers, and Slick moaned as soon as she took him into her mouth. Slick dropped the remainder of his burger back in the bag that was beside him and threw his head back and enjoyed the fire dome he was receiving.

"Gahhh damn babe," Slick moaned. He put his hand on Amanda's head and pushed it down as he fucked her mouth. Amanda seemed unbothered by his aggressiveness. The shit was superb, but he wasn't ready to bust just yet so he pushed her up and stepped out of his pants and polo boxers fully. Slick briefly thought about the fact that he didn't lock the door, but said fuck it because he knew nobody else was coming to visit. Amanda had on a peach sundress that clung to her body and he pulled it over her head. When he looked down he noticed that she didn't have on a bra or panties and he smiled.

"Panties don't go with sundresses," Amanda stated flirtatiously.

"Shiiidddd I ain't complaining," Slick replied and picked Amanda up and took her to his bedroom. He playfully threw her down on his king size bed and dove right between her legs. Slick teased Amanda's pearl and entered two fingers into her tightness. When his tongue began to work its magic, Amanda's body began to convulse. The moans that escaped her lips only turned him on that much more. After she came for the second time, Slick rose up and grabbed both of Amanda's legs. He spread them and put them over his shoulders, and then glided into her wetness.

Slick grinded into Amanda and the way that she was throwing it back at him made him almost cum. He wasn't ready to nut fast, so he flipped her over and entered her doggy style. Amanda cried out in pleasure and pain as Slick beat her pussy up. She wasn't able to match him thrust for thrust in that position and Slick smiled because he knew that he was wearing her down. A few minutes later, he felt her pussy pulsate and she cried out as she came. A few moments later, he tried to pull out of her, but the pussy was too good to pull out of.

"Damn girl… you tryna make me wife you up for real for real ain't ya?" Slick said as he fell down beside Amanda on the bed.

"That wouldn't be a bad thing would it," Amanda giggled and replied.

"Ion think it will… beauty, brains, and good pussy… shiiddd let's get it," he told her.

As they laid on the bed, Slick and Amanda took deep breaths to recapture much needed air as they recovered from their sexual workout that they just gave each other. A sound near the hallway captured their attention and made them looked towards the door. Their eyes widen with total surprise by a visitor standing at the entrance to the room.

"I sure as hell hope you enjoyed that pussy because it was your last sample," a voice heckled from the doorway.

Slick and Amanda looked up and all they saw was someone in all black with two guns in hand aimed at them.

"What the fuck?" Slick yelled while Amanda started crying hysterically.

***

"You done came in this bitch and turned shit around, but you know the hating is going on right?" Scott said to Tay during some down time while they were out on the yard.

"I'm prepared. Same shit goes on out there on the streets. Pussy ass niggas stay hating," Tay coolly replied.

For most niggas, the past six months probably would have been hell, but Tay was in prison and still calling shots. He considered himself to be a boss and he was still making boss moves in and outside of those four walls he was confined to. Having Kya at the prison with him was a blessing. She looked out for him in more ways than one and Kentay found himself wanting and actually needing her in major ways. The shit was strange to him because any of his other jump offs never crossed his mind like Kya. He sometimes daydreamed about her ass and wanted to slap his own ass back into reality. A very small part of him wondered what life would be like with Kya on the outside, but the other part of him knew that he was going for Ashanti because he wasn't a loser. He had a few thoughts of letting her go, but then the arrogant side of him always kicked in and he said fuck that, he was getting his wife back. The fact that Ahmad made his way down to check Tay still had him feeling some type of way, but he had to admit that he respected his style and the fact that he wasn't a punk.

"What up Tay? Can I make a call?" a dude that everybody called Tee walked up and asked. Kentay stared at the dude because he had never said two words to him before.

"I ain't got it," Tay replied.

When the guy turned to leave, Tay pulled out his phone and made a call, being sure to place it on speaker so the dude could hear. He smirked when Tee turned and glanced at him.

"Police ass nigga," Tay said loud enough for him to hear.

He chopped it up with Scott for a few more minutes and then made his exit because he was about to go and make a peanut butter and jelly sandwich. When Kentay rounded the corner, he heard some whispering but paid it no mind. After only three more steps, a blow to the back of the head caused him to stumble and fall forward. Before Tay could catch his balance, all he felt were kicks and punches to every part of his body. The only thing that he could do was cover his face, but that didn't last long because someone moved his hands and kicked him dead in the nose which was followed by more blows to his face. No matter how bad it hurt, he wouldn't allow himself to cry.

"Aye, aye… break it up,"

"Stand back! Everybody stand back!" another guard yelled. Tay heard a guard yelling in the distance. Footsteps could be heard coming his way, but one more kick to the face turned everything in his world black.

A couple of hours later, Kentay woke up in a white room. He tried to move and it felt like he had been hit by an eighteen-wheeler.

"Arrgghhh," he moaned.

"You're awake fast. With that ass whoopin' they put on you I figured you would be out quite a while," a woman stated. He turned his head to the left and noticed that the woman had on some scrubs, but her back was to him so he couldn't see her face. The voice sounded familiar to Kentay, but he couldn't place it for shit. He heard the same woman and a man talking about how he would be fine and to give him some Tylenol if needed for pain, and then a door slammed shortly afterwards.

"Can you sit up Mills?" a male voice asked.
Instead of answering, Kentay sat up. He grimaced from the pain a little, but he was determined to get the fuck up so that he could get out of whatever room he was in. Things started to come back to him and he realized that he had got jumped and must have ended up in the infirmary.

"I'm good… I can go back to my cell," Tay replied.

"Normally you would have to stay overnight, but you have a meeting with the Warden in a few hours," the man told him. "The nurse said you're good to go, so you can get outta here," he continued.

Kentay wasted no time getting up. He was in a hell of a lot of pain, but dared not let it show on his face. When the door opened, Tay walked out and made his way to his cell. The first face he saw along the way was Big Al, who held the same look every time he saw him.

"My reach is in, as well as, outta here. Learn that no means no," Big Al said and swiftly sauntered away before Kentay could even hit him with a reply.

He made it to his cell and received stares along the way. Each person that gazed at him, Kentay was sure to lock eyes with them and showed no fear. He saw Kya making her way over and went and met her. She had a look of panic on her face, but he gave her a look that let her know not to act soft around everyone. Kentay knew that niggas were jealous because of the relationship he had with Kya and he wasn't trying to get her fired or no shit like that.

"What in the hell happened?" she asked when he was close enough to her to whisper.

"Some pussy ass niggas jumped me, but it's all good. All them muthafucka's gon' have to see me," he replied through gritted teeth.

"Damn... I gotta get to shift report, but I'll be back," Kya told him and hurriedly left.

Kentay made it to his cell and went straight to the bathroom. When he looked in the mirror, he became angry. Just looking at his face had him seeing red. Although the pain felt far worse than it looked, the audacity of someone even thinking to put hands on him and acting on it was what pissed him off the most. He stood there and thought about all of the interactions that he had with Big Al and started putting two and two together.

"This nigga got rank, but what the fuck is his beef with me?" Tay mumbled to himself. He had no idea what the fuck was going on but had every intention on finding out. The first person on his list was Tee though. The vibe he felt when Tee asked for the phone was off, which was why he reacted in the manner that he did. Kentay had enough of the little pity party in the mirror, so he backed away and went and sat on the bed.

With both of his hands on his head, Tay closed his eyes and did something that he hadn't done in a long time... he prayed. He knew he wasn't the best nigga in the world, but he also knew he wasn't the worst. The feelings that he was having, he knew that he would fuck around and get life in that bitch if he reacted on them, so he prayed that God would give him another chance. He wanted to offer up a bargain but told himself that would be too cliché. Kentay looked up when he heard his name called.

"Mills! This way!" a male correctional officer called out to him.

Kentay slowly got up and followed him. He was being cautious because he knew that everyone was gunning for him and set-ups were real as hell. There weren't many people in their cells as Tay walked through, so he figured everyone was doing their own thing. He had no idea where he was being led to, but he followed anyway and wished that he had grabbed his razor just in case any bullshit was about to take place. After walking for what seemed like a mile, the officer opened a door and Kentay walked in and saw two old white men at a table. He couldn't tell what was going on by the looks on their faces, but he prepared himself for the worst.

"Have a seat Mr. Mills," one of the men spoke, and Kentay complied after the door slammed behind him. He was now alone with the two men and they stared at him like they wanted to kill him, but he played it cool. Kentay sat there and listened to them ramble on and on about criminals, cases, the law, and all types of shit, but he knew that they hadn't gotten to the meat of the conversation and was only prolonging the time. When they brought up his case, he finally gave them a little more attention because they started off by saying sometimes people are guilty, but when proper protocol isn't taken, things don't go as planned.

"We're going to have to let you go on a few technicalities. It may take a few days to get your paperwork processed, and the charge nurse has to come in here and say that you're medically fine in just a few minutes. Once you're cleared by her and the paperwork, you'll be a free man. I have a feeling that you'll be back," one of the men stated in which Kentay had learned was the Warden.

"Come again," Kentay spoke. "Did you just say that I was about to be released on some technicalities?" he asked, trying to hide his grin.

The Warden didn't want to repeat himself. The rubbing of his eyes, the slight eye roll, and the pinching of his chin were straight indications that he didn't want to say the words Mills and release again.

Letting out a deep sigh, the Warden confirmed his original statement. "Yes, Mills, you heard correctly. As much as I hate to do this, you will be released within the next couple of days as soon as your paperwork is ready," the Warden choked out.

"Alright, bet that!" Kentay muttered after getting clarification.

After hearing that he was going to be released, Kentay wanted to jump for joy, but he decided to act nonchalant. He didn't want to give them any indication that he was anxious as hell to get out of there. He said a silent "thank you God" as he realized the magnitude of getting a second chance outside of prison walls. Prayer really works Kentay silently mused to himself.

A few moments later, the door opened and in walked a nurse. "What the fuck? Courtney?!" Kentay exclaimed.

***

After months of turmoil, things were finally starting to look up for Ashanti. She wasn't able to take any summer classes because she had been too busy taking care of personal problems and getting her life back on track. Ashanti was loving the new her, but she couldn't shake the eerie feeling that some type of shit was about to pop off. The day was about to get busy, so Ashanti walked outside of her new town home to go and check the mail. Since she wanted to be free of Kentay, she moved out of the condo he had moved her into, traded the truck in for one a different color, and started living her life the way it needed to be lived. After searching and searching for a new place, she finally decided on The Block Townhomes that were located down South Montgomery.

Ashanti grabbed her mail and the first letter she saw was from her attorney. Her stomach was in knots because she hadn't heard from him in about a week or so and the last conversation hadn't gone the way that she had expected. Shanti walked back inside and checked on Kendra to make sure that she was still sleeping. When she saw that she was, she was elated because she would be alert for her birthday party that was taking place in just a few hours at McKee Park. Ashanti and Ahmad, along with Dennis, had been caring for Kendra because neither of them could bear the thought of her being shipped away to strangers. It was a very tough decision for Ashanti to make, but she prayed and felt like she was doing the right thing.

After taking a deep breath, Ashanti sat down on a barstool at the island and opened her mail. She read the contents of the letter and read everything again to be sure that she fully understood. When Ashanti realized that she was indeed not married to Kentay anymore, she screamed loudly and then jumped up quickly from the island. In her excitement, the barstool fell to the floor as she went to grab her phone to call Ahmad. Before she could place the call, she heard the door open and ran into Ahmad's arms when he entered. She automatically jumped on him, wrapped her legs around his waist, and started placing kisses all over his face. Ahmad didn't know what to make of her enthusiasm. Not that he mind any of it. Finally, getting her to place where she could talk, Ahmad asked Ashanti what was going on.

"You okay babe? I heard you screaming," he stated with concern etched in his voice while looking around.

"I'm great!! Come look at this," she exclaimed and pulled him to the kitchen.
As soon as she handed Ahmad the letter, she heard Kendra whining and went to go and get her. By the time she made it to the room, Kendra was scooting down on the side of the bed. Ashanti scooped her up and gave her a few kisses on the jaw, which caused her to giggle.

"Tee Tee," Kendra cooed.
Instead of allowing Kendra to call her mama, like she had started saying, Ashanti taught her to say Tee Tee. She loved the little girl, but she didn't want to confuse her in any type of way. Ashanti knew that the truth always came out in situations like that, and she didn't want Kendra to feel like she has been misled all of her life. Ashanti made her way back into the kitchen and bumped into a smiling Ahmad.

"I told you everything was going to work out," Ahmad told Ashanti.

"Mad," Kendra said and reached for Ahmad.
Ashanti put her down and made her take a few steps toward Ahmad. Her actual birthday was the day before and she had taken her first step. The excitement Ashanti and Ahmad showed made Kendra keep taking steps. Ashanti watched her take a few steps and then Ahmad scooped her up.

"Hey uncle's little baby," Ahmad said and loved on Kendra.

"You happy?" he asked Ashanti.

"Happy is an understatement," Shanti cheerfully beamed.
When Kentay never replied to the divorce papers that Ashanti sent, she took matters into her own hands. After researching for days and

weeks, Ashanti found an attorney out of Tupelo that would take on her case. Google had told her that when a spouse is incarcerated, a divorce could be granted after six months, but there were chances that it may take longer. Ashanti wanted to be free of Kentay because the longer that she carried his name; it meant that she was also legally responsible for him. It was enough that she was taking care of his child, but she didn't want to be obligated to do anything for him if any type of situation may have come about. The fact that Kentay had drugged her helped her case, and now she was Ashanti McNeal and Kentay didn't even know that the divorce was finalized without him.

"We got everything set up at the park and dad is on his way here to change clothes," Ahmad stated.

"Great... let me ask you something," Ashanti replied.

"Go ahead," he told her.

"Do you regret any of this?" Ashanti asked and nodded her head towards Kendra.

"Babe... we've been through this time and time again. I'm good. We good. Everything is good," he said. Ashanti watched him sit Kendra down on the couch and then came her way.

"I just don't want any issues on down the line. This is a big responsibility and you have a promising career ahead of..."she started saying but Ahmad cut her off by kissing her sensually.

"We don't know what the future holds, but I can tell you now that I'm good. This entire situation is crazy, but I love you, and that little girl right there has my blood. What kind of human being would I be to treat you differently for having a heart of gold," Ahmad told her.

"I love you so much. I hate some of the shit that happened in my life, but it only makes me appreciate you more," Ashanti replied to him.

A knock at the door interrupted them from their conversation. Ahmad went and opened the door and his dad walked in. He spoke to Ashanti and then went straight to Kendra. Ashanti watched him pick Kendra up and spin her around. That little girl had everyone wrapped around her fingers and toes. They talked about the party and how it was such a beautiful day and then got dressed to leave. Ashanti dressed Kendra in a custom made Minnie Mouse tee from Just an Xpression and a little tutu. Each of them had tee shirts with their names on the back. They all wanted to make Kendra's first birthday memorable despite the fact that both of her parents were absent.

The party started at noon and was ending by two o'clock. Kids from daycare, along with Aaliyah, Seth, and a few of Ahmad's friends were in attendance. The cake by Kita's Kakes was to die for. It was made with love and it was so good that none was left to take home. Chiquita Porter even threw in a small cake for Kendra to play in, but she didn't destroy it as expected. The guys were deflating all of the bouncers while the girls were cleaning up in preparation to leave. Dennis was taking Kendra back to Jackson with him for a few days and Shanti and Liyah were about to go and watch their men ball out in a tournament. Everyone was pleased with how the day had gone so far.

***

Ahmad and Seth decided that they would play in a pickup tournament that was hosted by the a few people in the community. They knew that most athletes didn't play outside of the gym, but being active in the community was something the two of them had always done. Ahmad and Seth rode over to the West Side Park together while Ashanti and Aaliyah made a run to store to grab Powerade's for them. It was a hot day in August, which was why Dennis had decided to take his granddaughter with him. Dennis had a few reservations about him playing, but he allowed both of them to make their own decisions.

Around five o'clock that evening, Ahmad's team was undefeated after the current game ended. He walked over to where Shanti and Liyah were sitting in chairs and grabbed his drink from her that she was holding out for him.

"Thanks baby," he told her after almost drinking the entire bottle in one gulp.

"Gotta keep my baby hydrated out there," Shanti told him and got up and wiped his sweat off with the towel she was holding.

"We bout to walk down here to the bathroom before the next game start," Ahmad told Ashanti.

"Okay… me and Liyah will be right behind y'all," Shanti replied.

Ahmad walked off and him and Seth started talking shit to each other. He saw a red Jeep Cherokee driving down the road slow but paid it no mind. When him and Seth made it beside a Black Suburban, shots rang out and Ahmad promptly fell to the ground. Blood covered his white shirt and deafening screams could be heard throughout the park.

Ashanti and Liyah immediately sprinted towards Ahmad and Seth. They couldn't believe what the hell just happened. As Ashanti got closer to Ahmad, she saw all the blood that was oozing from his body. As soon as she reached him, Ashanti dropped to her knees and tried to put pressure everywhere to stop the bleeding. She didn't know exactly where he was shot, but all she wanted was for the bleeding to stop. She started panicking and started to cry and scream frantically.

"Ahmad, baby I'm here! Just hold on ok. Everything's gon' be alright! You hear me! Everything's gon' be alright. I love you ok. You hear me. We love each other. Don't you dare fucking leave me Ahmad," Ashanti demanded with a lot of hostility. "Come on baby! You can do this. Just look at me ok, I got you. Baby, I got you. You gon be alright. Just hold on. Can you do that for me? Just hold baby. I love you baby," she continued to beg and plead with Ahmad.

Ashanti was scared out of her mind, and she wanted to do everything in her powers to will him to just hold on. She realized how her instincts were on point in this matter. Just when everything was looking up for her, Ahmad, and their lives together, this shit happened. She was on the verge of losing the true love of her life, but she couldn't let that happen. Ashanti shook her head as a way to clear her mind from negative thoughts and decided to remain positive. No way was she about to lose Ahmad after all the shit they have gone through to be together. However, her frenzy went through the roof when she saw Ahmad's eyes closing.

"NOOOOOOO OH MY GOD!!! NOOOOO!!!! Stay with me baby!! Stay…with… me!" Ashanti screamed as her heart was breaking. "Ahmad baby, listen to me. Open your eyes. Please baby. Open your eyes. Open your got damn eyes! NOW AHMAD! Oh God, Oh God, Oh God! NO! NO! NO! NO! NOOOOO!!" she tearfully and grimly yelled over and over again. Of all the yelling and screaming that were heard in park, Ashanti's solemn voice could be heard over everyone's.

***

Ahmad never thought that the day would end like it did. When he thought about his future, it was always with Ashanti and playing somewhere in the NBA. It never crossed his mind that something of this caliber could happen. As he lay on the ground bleeding, he reflected over his life and thought about his dad, his sister, and Ashanti. He couldn't believe that he had gotten so lucky and blessed to find the woman that was made for him. As darkness started to close in, Ahmad was thankful that he had gotten the chance to find love and let love find him. He heard Ashanti's beautiful voice demanding and begging him to stay alive. He could feel her heart breaking because his was breaking as well. That wasn't how it was supposed to end. His life wasn't supposed to take the path that it had spiraled down. But yet still, he was lying on a hard cold ground in an unbelievable shock, but still trying to fight. He was trying his best to stay alive. As he gazed towards Ashanti and heard her frightening screams, Ahmad tried to tell her that everything was okay and that he loved her. However, he couldn't form any words as his eyes started to close and he began to choke on his own blood.

To Be Continued…

Chapter One

Sirens sounded in the distance and people were in shock, running and screaming as Ashanti cried out uncontrollably for Ahmad not to leave her. She was in such a state of shock that she didn't even realize that she had been pulled away from Ahmad so that a few people could perform CPR before the ambulance arrived. Everything was a blur to Ashanti. She never saw the paramedic's park and rush over to assist Ahmad. When she heard someone say "Hurry, he's lost a lot of blood and we're losing him" she lost it. It took Seth, Aaliyah, and a few other people to keep her away from Ahmad so that the paramedics could tend to him. Ashanti watched through tears as they loaded Ahmad onto a stretcher and rushed towards the awaiting ambulance. She broke away and rushed over to hop in, but one of the paramedics informed her that she couldn't ride.

"What the fuck you mean I can't ride?" Shanti screamed in frustration.

"Shanti, we can follow them. Come on so they can work on him," Liyah said in a panic and pulled her away.

Ashanti felt Aaliyah as she pulled her towards the car. She heard Seth yelling and cussing and fussing about a red jeep and telling them to hurry up. The cops had arrived on the scene and were asking bystanders questions as they tried to piece together everything that had transpired. Bullets had hit a few other people, so the cops assumed that it was a random drive by. When they reached the truck, Ashanti finally realized that they were getting into Seth's ride with him instead of her truck. Aaliyah hopped in the back with Ashanti, and Seth took off before the door was closed all of the way. Shanti looked down at her clothes and saw the red blood stains from when she had been holding Ahmad. She broke down crying at the sight, sobbing hard at how the day's events had ended. Unable to do anything else, Liyah pulled her in for a hug and told her that she had to be strong for Ahmad. Ashanti shook her head *yes*, but her tears never stopped flowing.

"Where the fuck are they going? We just passed the hospital!" Shanti looked up and exclaimed with extreme irritation as they bypassed Oktibbeha County Hospital.

"I don't know, but I'm right on they asses," Seth replied as he followed behind the ambulance and ran the red light on North Jackson Street.

Twenty minutes later, they turned into Baptist Memorial Hospital in Columbus right behind the ambulance. Before Seth was completely parked, Ashanti hopped out of his truck and took off running. When she made it to the doors, she had no idea where they had rushed Ahmad to. The EMTs were moving at the speed of lightening. Ashanti heard a doctor being paged to the emergency room as she ran up to the receptionist and told them why she was there.

"I'm with the man they just rushed in here. He was shot. What's going on? Can I go to the back?" Ashanti spoke nonstop and didn't give the girl time to answer her.

"Calm down sweetheart… I'll find out as much as I can, but I know you can't go back there right now," the girl told her.

As soon as the receptionist finished talking and before Shanti could ask any more questions, Liyah jogged up and stood beside her.

"We'll be right over there," Liyah told the lady and pulled Ashanti with her to some chairs that were in the corner.

"He can't die… he just can't die. Shit wasn't supposed to happen like this," Ashanti said a few minutes after she sat down.

"My boy ain't gon die," Seth said as he walked over and paced the floor. Neither of them knew that he had made it inside until he spoke those words.

"Someone needs to call Mr. Jones," Liyah stated.

"Shit!" Shanti and Seth exclaimed in unison because neither of them had thought to call Ahmad's dad and tell him what was going on. Everything happened so fast, and they were in a state of shock.

"I don't know where the hell my phone is! I wonder if he had left Starkville yet," Shanti stated in a panic.

"It's right here," Liyah said and pulled it out of her purse.

"Thanks girl! You're a lifesaver," Shanti expressed as she grabbed her iPhone from her friend.

Ashanti tried to gather her thoughts before she placed the call. Nothing she thought of sounded good, so she went ahead and dialed the number, and Dennis picked up after it rang three times.

Shanti opened her mouth to talk, but the only thing she got out was his name.

"Ahmad..." she stated barely above a whisper.

"Did they win the tournament? I just got on the road about thirty minutes ago," Dennis inquired with a chuckle.

"Yes, but..." Ashanti replied as she tried to find the words to admit that Ahmad had been shot. She took a deep breath before continuing to break the news to Dennis. "Well... something happened, and you need to come to the hospital in Columbus immediately," Ashanti replied barely above a whisper.

"Something happened? What do you mean something happened? What the hell happened to my boy?" Dennis vocalized with a hint of fear in his voice.

"I'm sorry...I'm so sorry, but Ahmad was shot" she cried as she was overcome with emotions.

"Shot? Did you say he was shot?" Dennis questioned with total disbelief. Ashanti couldn't answer his first question because he rapidly started quizzing her about what the hell happened at the tournament.

When Dennis started firing off questions back to back to back, Ashanti became overwhelmed and was on the brink of tears again. Seth grabbed the phone from her and talked to Dennis. When he finished, he handed Shanti her phone back, and they all sat there in silence for a few minutes with their own thoughts running rapid through their minds.

"I'm glad y'all finally made up Shanti. My boy really loves you. He gon pull through, you just gotta be there for him aight," Seth stated with firmness.

"You best believe I ain't goin' nowhere... no matter what!" Shanti replied.

"Damn we shoulda listened to Mr. D and not played street ball. Dammit," Seth vented.

"It's not y'all fault that people don't know how to act. Don't blame yourself babe," Liyah said as she left Ashanti's side to go and comfort Seth. "You just said that he's gonna be okay, and he is. We all gotta stay strong," Liyah continued as she offered encouraging words.

As they sat there talking and comforting each other, breaking news came across the TV that was on in the corner near them and Seth's phone began ringing simultaneously.

"Mississippi State's basketball star Ahmad Jones has been shot while playing in a community basketball tournament right here at West Side Park. We have been told that he is currently in surgery at Baptist Memorial Hospital, but the extent of his injuries is unknown at this time. One source has leaked that things are currently touch and go so Jones is in our prayers. The basketball star recently lost his mom. No suspects are in custody for the shooting and if anyone has any information please call the Starkville Police Department at 662-323-," the reporter stated, but everyone's attention shifted to the doors when reporters busted through the doors.

Security was called over the intercom to report to the emergency room and within minutes, the entire waiting room was full.

"What the hell?" Ashanti asked no one in particular. They looked on as security tried to get everything under control. One of the reporters looked over and pointed at Seth and then headed towards them. As all of the commotion played out, Code Red was announced, and everyone behind the desk went into a frenzy. Everything and everyone moved so fast, and Ashanti found herself hyperventilating, and the next thing she knew, all she saw was black.
***

"He was hit three times. One bullet to the leg, one to the neck that went in and out, and the most dangerous one went through his side. It's lodged right next to his spinal cord. We know that it's risky, but we have to do surgery right away," the doctor stated with a high degree of urgency.

"I'll go out and see if there's a next of kin that can give us the okay, if not, it's your call," one of the nurses stated.

"Just get the bullet out of me right now so I can get up and go home," Ahmad thought he was saying out loud, but he was only talking in his head. He listened as the doctors continued to talk and prepare him for surgery. All he could think about was how everything was just all good, and now he was lying in the hospital with a bullet lodged in him that could possibly paralyze him. Ahmad had no idea who else had been shot or if anyone had died. He told himself that whoever was responsible was going to have to pay for all of the turmoil that they had caused. Ahmad heard a Code Red as it was called, and one of the doctors updated staff that the patient next door had gone into cardiac arrest.

"The patient's dad is on the way. But the friend called him, and he gave the okay to do anything necessary. It's a circus out there because reports have circulated that Mr. Jones might be dead. His girlfriend just had an anxiety attack and passed out," the nurse came back in and announced.

"Tell my baby I'm gon be alright," Ahmad voiced in his head.

A few minutes later, he heard the doctors saying that they were about to proceed with surgery. The anesthesiologist was called in to put Ahmad completely under, and he heard someone saying to not give him a full dose. The last words he heard were "he'll be fine" before everything turned white.

Chapter Two

"Why are you here?" Slick asked with no fear as one gun was aimed directly at him.

"You keep picking everyone over me, and I apologized to you a million times. What does this bitch have that I don't?" Lena asked as she took the gun off of Slick and aimed both of them at Amanda, who looked back and forth between the two with an expression of confusion on her face.

"Lena... Don't do any fuck shit okay? If you kill her, Ima kill you and that mean you still gon fuckin' lose," Slick replied with agitation etched in his voice.

"So even with a gun pointed at this bitch, and one at you, you still gon pick her over me Slick?" Lena asked as tears started to stream down her face and shifted one gun back at him.

"Lena we been over, so I don't know why the fuck you even here," Slick replied as he shook his head and shifted towards the edge of the bed a little.

"Stop moving!" Lena threatened and stepped closer towards Slick with both guns shaking in her hands.

"Baby don't be mean to her. She has two guns pointed in our direction," Amanda finally found her voice and spoke.

Slick sat there quietly for a few minutes as he contemplated what Amanda had just verbalized. He didn't give a fuck about Lena's feelings, but he didn't want to see Amanda hurt in any type of way. As he stared into Lena's eyes, he could tell that she was a loose cannon. One would have thought that he was the one who did her wrong with the way that she was acting, but it was the complete opposite. She was the one who had smashed the homie behind Slick's back and more than one time.

"Let's talk Lena. Is that what you want?" Slick asked her as nicely as he could muster.

"Talk now. I'm listening. You want me or her?" Lena asked as she side eyed Amanda.

"Yes, Lena. I want you," Slick retorted.

"You really mean it? Don't just be saying shit to keep me from killing this bitch?" Lena said with venom laced in every word.

"Of course I do. Come give me a hug," Slick told her.

"Fuck me in front of this bitch then," Lena demanded.

Slick bit the inside of his jaw to keep from cussing Lena out. He sat there not knowing how much longer he was going to be able to take her bullshit. Slick looked at Amanda through his peripheral vision and could tell that she was getting pissed off by the way that she was biting her tongue. The one and only time that she had been upset with him was when she found out about the history he had with Kya. He knew that she had a hot temper at that very moment, but she did well at keeping it hidden. Judging by the look on her face, Amanda was almost at her breaking point, and he knew that he needed to do something.

"Let's do it then," Slick replied and stood up. Slick noticed the look of satisfaction on Lena's face as they made their way closer to each other. As Slick stood and was getting ready to pull Lena towards him, Amanda jumped up quickly at the same time. Lena fired a shot, but the push Amanda gave her caused Lena to stumble, which changed the direction of the gun just in time.

"You stupid bitch!" Amanda screamed as she jumped down on her and delivered blow after blow like she wasn't butt naked. Slick looked on as Amanda beat Lena to a bloody pulp. He had no desire to stop her. He felt like Lena deserved the beat down after the shit that she had just pulled. Slick went and grabbed a pair of shorts out of his drawer and slid them on.

"Call the cops and have this bitch arrested!" Amanda yelled at Slick after she was out of breath and satisfied with taking care of Lena.

"We don't deal with the cops round these parts babe. Calm down," Slick replied.

"This bitch just had guns pointed at both of our heads. You can call the fuckin' cops or I will!" Amanda screamed at Slick as she headed to the living room after she kicked Lena again and made her cry out in agony.

"Fuck!" Slick said to himself. He hated dealing with pigs, but he knew Amanda was right. He heard a knock on the door and headed towards it to answer it. However, before he was completely out of his room, a shot was fired, and he felt a stinging sensation in his right leg.

"Arrggghhh!" he yelled out in pain. A couple more shots were fired, but they hit the walls. At the same time, the cops had made their way inside. Slick cursed himself for not removing the guns away from the floor beside Lena. He thought that she was unconscious; but evidently she wasn't because she had just shot his ass.

Amanda ran to Slick's side yelling and screaming as two cops apprehended Lena before she could grab the other gun. It was then that Slick realized that Lena had actually shot him twice. The floor was covered in blood, and he heard Amanda along with one of the cops talking about calling 911. Slick didn't feel any pain in his side until after he saw that he had been shot. He was losing blood at a fast pace and for some reason, he felt himself becoming dizzy. The last thing he heard before passing out was Amanda screaming his name.

Four hours later, Slick woke up at Oktibbeha County Hospital, and Amanda was standing right beside his bed. He looked to his left and saw that he was hooked up to an IV and also noticed an empty bag of blood. Before he could ask any questions, Amanda spoke up.

"Hey babe, how are you feeling? You're fine. Thank God. No major damage to anything. Both were flesh wound shots. Thank God that trifling bitch can't shoot for shit. But, anyways… They just gave you some blood because it's standard because you lost some, and they are hydrating you with the fluids as a precaution. The doctor said you'll probably only have to stay overnight," Amanda informed him.

"I ain't staying in this bitch overnight. They got me fucked up," Slick retorted.

"Yes, you are. We gotta make sure you're fine. Oh and they arrested that bitch. You got any more secrets that I need to know about because that's two strikes right there," Amanda chided and then made him aware of everything that had gone on while he was incoherent.

"Those weren't secrets… them was just crazy situations from the past that's been over. Stop playing, you know I don't love them hoes," Slick replied. He glanced up at the TV and saw breaking news and his mouth flew open. Slick asked Amanda to turn the volume up because he didn't see the remote.

As soon as she granted his request, Slick listened as the reporter talked about a shooting that happened at West Side Park earlier that evening. He was ready to kick his own ass as the details unfolded and he put two and two together. It was reported that Ahmad Jones, along with a few other people had been shot while playing basketball. Slick knew that Ahmad and Kentay weren't on the best terms, but that was his brother who had been shot and according to the report and how everything played out, Slick knew who was responsible.

"Got dammit! I can't believe this! This bullshit is my fault," Slick said to himself.

"What's your fault babe?" Amanda inquired.

"I just gotta get outta here. I'm not staying here. I'm good," Slick said and sat up.

Slick continued to beat himself up about what had just gone down. He was starting to think that Buck wasn't in the house and had retaliated almost instantly. Slick thought about how he had parked his truck over at the park as a decoy and wondered if Buck had just did a drive by because his vehicle was there. The more he sat there and thought about it, the more it began to make sense. He needed to get the fuck up out of the hospital and make some moves so that he could figure out exactly what happened and what kind of vehicle was spotted. If it was that red jeep, he knew what the deal was.

"Where my phone at?" Slick asked with some urgency.

"I guess it's at home. You were eating when I came remember?" Amanda replied.

"Yeah you right. That's the more reason I gotta get outta here. I turned that shit on silent after I made it to the crib," Slick retorted as he pulled the IV out of his arm and stood up.

"So you just gon leave here for real?" Amanda shockingly inquired.

"Hell yeah! You said they gave me blood, and these fluids are just precautionary because it's only a flesh wound and shit. I'll drink some Gatorade or some shit and get replenished," Slick said as he looked around.

"Where my clothes at though?" he continued.

"You clothes are all bloody so they put them in a bag, and I just threw them away," Amanda responded.

"Well look like my ass bout to be out as I leave this bitch because I ain't staying. Let's go," Slick demanded and headed towards the door as he limped a little and pulled the hospital gown closer to his body. He saw Amanda shake her head, but she followed him without protesting any further.

When Slick walked out of the room, he bumped into a nurse and before she could open her mouth to say anything, he gave her a death stare. The lady rushed off and he took that as his sign to go ahead and leave. He could tell by the look on her face that she was going to tell someone what was going on.

"Where you park at?" Slick inquired.

"Right outside the door. I wasn't gonna move out of emergency until they moved you to a room," Amanda replied.

"Cool... speed up," he told her as he proceeded forward.

"Hey hey... wait a minute. You can't leave," Slick heard a lady calling out behind them.

He ignored her and sped up his pace as much as he could as he held onto his side and grimaced a little. Once he hit the button and made it through the double doors, his fast paced walk turned into a slight jog. Since it was just a flesh wound, he was able to continue forward with just a little bit of pain. He could hear Amanda jiggling the keys behind him as they passed by the receptionist who was talking on the phone. The way she was laughing, he knew that it was a personal call that she was on and silently thanked her. As soon as they made it outside, Slick saw Amanda's car and made it to it in less than a minute. She hit the locks with her remote and he got into the driver seat. The same nurse made it outside when he crunk up, but he ignored her and left without looking back.

"You crazy as hell! I can't believe you just left the damn hospital AMA," Amanda told him and she started laughing while shaking her head.

"Well believe it baby. I ain't got time to be sitting up in no hospital," Slick replied as he headed towards his place. "Our night just been fucked up, but I promise Ima make it up to you," he told her.

"It has been crazy, but I'm just glad that you're okay. I'm definitely gon let you make it up to me though," Amanda retorted.

Slick made it to his place in ten minutes. When he parked Amanda's car, he told her that he was only going in to grab some clothes and they would go and stay at The Hilton. He had been thinking about moving, and now he knew that it was really time because he was sure that his neighbors would be watching closely because of all of the shit that had gone down. Amanda told him that when the first shot was fired, one of the neighbors called the cops and that was how they had gotten their so fast. Slick was thankful for that because he was sure that someone would have ended up dead otherwise and he damn sure didn't want it to be him.

After gathering a couple of outfits, his car keys and a Corona out of the fridge, Slick limped into his living room and picked his cell phone up from the end table where he had placed it earlier that evening. As soon as he hit the home button, he saw that he had over a dozen missed calls. A few were from Dub, one was from one of the other homies, but the majority was from Kentay.

"What the fuck done happened now?" Slick said because he knew anytime Kentay called back to back it was something important.

Chapter Three

"Good even gentlemen. Hi Mr. Mills," Courtney spoke when she walked in.

"Good evening, Ms. Courtney," the warden replied and looked back and forth between Courtney and Kentay with a look that showed he was trying to figure out the connection. Courtney ignored him and got right on down to business.

"I have reviewed all of the charts, and Mr. Mills needs just a few more tests done before I can clear him. Head injuries are something serious, as you all know, so we have to be sure. I have them scheduled for Tuesday, and the results should be in on Thursday or Friday. If everything is clear, Mr. Mills will be free to go," Courtney stated.

Kentay glared at her and if looks could kill she would be as dead as a door knob. He knew that was her voice from earlier, but thought his mind was playing tricks on him. It took everything in Kentay for him not to get up choke the shit out of Courtney as he sat there and thought about the foul ass shit that she had done to him.

A few years before Kentay pursued and conquered Ashanti, there was Courtney Lynn Thomas. Courtney was the love of Kentay's life throughout his teenage and the beginning of his adult years, until she did the unforgivable sin in his eyes. Before Kentay became heavy in the streets, it was Courtney who he spent all of his time with. You hardly ever saw one without the other. Kentay knew that she was going to be his wife one day. She wanted to graduate from college and start her career before getting married, which was why Kentay hadn't locked her in yet. She cooked for him and Slick after they played basketball in the evenings. And when Kentay broke into the game, Courtney even helped him out with anything he asked.

One day Courtney came to Kentay with tears streaming down her face, crying that her life was over, and she didn't know what she was going to do.

"What's wrong babe? Who I gotta fuck up?" Tay asked her.

"I... fucked... up," Courtney sobbed.

"Calm down and tell me what's wrong," Kentay said as he pulled her in close.

"I missed a couple of my pills and now… now I'm… pregnant," Courtney continued to cry.

"Pregnant? Did you just say you pregnant?" Tay inquired.

"Yes," Courtney replied.

Kentay got up and picked Courtney up and spun her around. He had the biggest smile plastered on his face as Courtney fought for him to put her down. Kentay ignored her pleas and continued to celebrate until she continued with her yelling and screaming and started hitting him.

"Why you crying? We can take care of a baby," Tay retorted after he put her down.

"I wanna finish school and have a steady job, and be married before I have a baby Tay. You ain't ready for no baby and neither am I," Courtney responded.

"What the fuck you mean? Ain't nobody ever really just ready for babies, the shit just happen. We'll be fine. Stop stressing and shit," Tay told her.

"I'm not keeping this baby Tay. I just can't," Courtney tried to reason with him.

"Courtney… if you take your ass to an abortion clinic and kill my baby, Ima fuck you up. And that's real," Tay calmly but firmly told her.

'It's my body Kentay. You can't make that decision for me," Courtney fired back.

"Is it my baby?" Kentay inquired.

"What kinda question is that? You know it's yours," she replied.

"Well I can make whatever decision I want. Don't kill my fuckin' baby. I'll have somebody watching every got damn women's clinic in a thousand mile radius. Try it if you want to," Tay told her and walked off.

Kentay was pissed the fuck off when he left Courtney. He couldn't believe she had the audacity to want to have an abortion like he wouldn't be there for her and their baby. From the moment they made everything official years ago, they had been there for one another and worked through everything. Kentay worshipped the ground Courtney walked on, and there was really absolutely nothing that he wouldn't do for her. Many females tried to get at him, but his attention was only on Courtney and the streets. He was dead serious about having people watch every facility. There was no way he was going to allow Courtney to kill his seed.

Three days passed before Kentay calmed down a little and finally reached out to Courtney. She had been calling him, but he ignored each call. When she texted and he realized that she was only trying to plead her case, he continued to dismiss her. Finally, he decided that he would go to her house and talk some sense into her face to face. He would never stand in the way of her accomplishing her goals. However, he just wanted her to know that he had her back one hundred percent.

Since it was the Thursday, he knew that she was home alone since her mom was a traveling nurse and came in on Friday evenings. Kentay knocked on the door, but Courtney never replied or opened it. He knew that she had to be home, so he walked around back where they had a spare key under the flower pot and let himself in through the back door.

"Courtney! Where you at babe?" he called out to her.

When he heard some faint moans, he sped up his pace and headed to the back where Courtney's room was. The sight he saw before him caused his heart to skip a beat. Courtney was laying on the floor in a puddle of blood with tears flowing down her cheeks. He could tell that she was in some excruciating pain by her facial expressions and the searing moans that escaped her lips.

"What the fuck happened?" Kentay asked as he rushed to Courtney's side. She never uttered a word. Before Kentay picked her up, he started looking around the room. When he noticed what was going on, he stood up and glared at Courtney like he was about to kill her with his bare hands.

"The Hell? Did you really just lay here and perform an at home abortion Courtney? A fucking clothes hanger, vinegar, what the fuck?" Kentay sadly inquired with total disbelief in his voice. He was pissed the fuck off, but sadness took over his emotions. "Answer me dammit!" Kentay shouted, unable to keep his feelings at bay.

"I'm sorry... I just couldn't," Courtney sobbed through her tears.

"Sorry! Sorry! That's some straight bullshit Courtney! You didn't want my baby that fucking bad, so you decided to take care of the it your damn self? And now, you're supposedly... sorry. Your muthafuckin' ass ain't fucking sorry about shit. Oh my bad... yeah, *you're sorry your muthafuckin' ass got caught. That's what the fuck you're sorry about. You knew what in the hell you were doing. You told me that you didn't want my baby. But, I didn't think your stupid ass would be this brazen to do a home abortion."* Kentay argued with total disgust for his woman...ex-woman. *"You were my first love Courtney. You knew there was nothing I wouldn't do for you, but for you to be so fuckin' selfish like this... I can't deal wit' it. You're fuckin' dead to me. You hear me? Dead! Don't bring your two-faced ass around me again. Love don't live here anymore"* Kentay told her and walked away without looking back. He heard her calling his name, but he refused to stop because what she had done was inexcusable in his eyes.

"I just need to take him to get his vitals again, and I'll set the testing up and keep check on him until his departure," Kentay heard Courtney tell the warden and snapped out of his reverie.

Emotions that he thought were long gone resurfaced and Kentay's eyes closed as tears were on the brink. He refused to let them fall, especially in front of someone who was so selfish and in his mind caused him to be the way he was. After Courtney killed his seed, he swore off women and dumped them all into the same category. When he met Ashanti, there was something very special about her, but he wouldn't allow himself to fall completely in love with her for the fear that she would hurt him. He loved her, but he had limits on his love. He justified Courtney's actions as the reason why he fucked around. The day Ashanti was about to have the abortion, all he could think about was Courtney, and to him, it confirmed that all women were the same. If he could turn back the hands of time, he would do a lot of shit different, but that wasn't possible, so he never dwelled on the shoulda, coulda, woulda's.

"Let's go Mills," Courtney said as she opened the door.

Kentay got up and followed her while trying to figure out what type of games she was playing now.

Chapter Four

It was well after midnight when the doctor finally came out and spoke to the Jones family. A nurse had been out and talked to them two times before, but she never answered the questions that everyone had directly. The vague answers she had given made everyone more nervous than they already were. Ashanti was given a shot for anxiety, and the nurse wanted to keep her in a room, but she refused because she wanted to be with everyone else.

Ahmad's doctor finally made it to the waiting room, where all of Ahmad's loved ones were waiting for an update on his injuries. He called out for Ahmad's family to make sure they were the right people. They nodded their heads in unison to indicate they were Ahmad's folk and waited for the doctor to continue.

"Hello, I'm Dr. Brandon, and I was the surgeon who worked on Ahmad. Will you guys follow me please?" the doctor stated more than asked.

Ashanti, Dennis, Seth, Aaliyah, and the basketball coach, who came to check on things, all hesitantly got up and followed the doctor. Tina made it to the hospital about two hours prior. She stayed seated and held Kendra, who had fallen asleep. Ashanti felt like they were about to get some bad news, so she started praying harder as they walked. Once the doctor reached a door that was labeled Chapel, Ashanti's heart sank. She watched the expressions on everyone's faces and could tell that everyone had similar thoughts, but they all remained quiet.

Everyone filed into the room where there were two couches, three round tables with chairs, a few recliners, and plenty of pamphlets and bibles placed everywhere. The doctor asked everyone to take a seat, but no one budged. That gave him the indication to go ahead and say what he had to say, so he paused for a moment before he started talking.

"The bullet that was lodged into the patient's back was removed, but we won't know the status of paralysis, if any, until he wakes up. We had to place him in what we call a medically induced coma because he had a seizure during surgery. That's not uncommon; he may have had a bad reaction to the anesthesia. We really won't know everything until all of his levels are back to normal. We anticipate a full recovery, but we must warn you to prepare for the worst," the doctor told them.

"Sounds like you just delivered us a bunch of bullshit with some missing pieces doc... what exactly are you saying?" Seth raised his voice and asked.

"That's what I'm tryna figure out too," Ashanti nervously stated as she let out a deep breath that she didn't realize she had been holding.

"I'm sure the great doctor here isn't leaving out any valuable information. Right doc? Because last I checked, my son has never had a seizure," Dennis chimed in.

"Calm down everyone... I've only spoke on facts, but if anything changes, I will be the one to let you all know," Dr. Brandon firmly stated.

"I'm definitely gonna hold you to that... Dr. Brandon," Dennis replied while looking at his name and picture on his badge.

The doctor talked for a few more minutes and told them that they could visit Ahmad in a little while, but only two at a time. Dennis agreed to let Ashanti and his coach visit first so coach could leave since it was so late. Ashanti wanted to be last, so she encouraged Seth to go with their coach. A few minutes later, a nurse came and told them that they could start visiting. Seth and the coach immediately got up and followed behind her. Ashanti sat there with her eyes closed, fighting sleep and praying.

"Shanti you know you need to get some rest like the nurse told you after giving you that shot," Liyah told her.

"I'm fine. I'm not leaving here without Ahmad so everyone might as well chill out," Shanti replied with her eyes still closed.

"Ahmad needs you strong boo. The least you can do is take a nap after you see him, okay," Liyah pleaded with her friend.

"I just gotta make sure he's okay, and then I'll be okay," Shanti replied in a voiced laced with exhaustion and fatigue.

"I understand. Ahmad is gonna be just fine. No matter what that doctor said or didn't say, Ahmad is a fighter and he will pull through," Liyah sincerely stated. They chatted for a few more minutes while everyone checked on Ahmad.

Ashanti was the last one to go and visit with Ahmad. She made her way to the room that he occupied and paused at the door before she went inside. She knew that it was imperative for her to be strong, so she took a deep breath and said another prayer before she went inside. When she finally walked in, her heart sank to see him just lying there not moving. However, she willed her feet to continue forward until she reached him. Ashanti grabbed Ahmad's hand and squeezed it gently. Besides the bandage that was on the left side of Ahmad's neck, he appeared to be sleeping peacefully. The rest of his body was covered up so no scars were visible. Ashanti stood there for a few minutes while trying to gather her thoughts and words to say.

"I don't know if you can hear me or not, but I pray that you can. If you can hear, I know you probably been waiting on me, but I had to let everyone else visit first and come last. Please fight baby! Don't leave me! I need you! You're the best thing that ever happened to me, baby. Please wake up Ahmad! The doctors are talking crazy, but you're going to the NBA like you always wanted. The whole world is pulling for you. You should see all of the reporters and people who have been trying to get back here to see you. Everyone needs you baby," Ashanti spoke to Ahmad while holding his hand as tears rolled freely down her face. She bent down and gave him a kiss and expected him to reciprocate.

"Wake up baby… pleeaasseee wake up!!" Ashanti pleaded while crying and sobbing uncontrollably. She had held it together as best as she could, but lost it when she never felt Ahmad squeeze her hand, kiss her back, or give her any sign that he was aware of her presence.

"Ma'am… we are going to have to ask you to leave," a nurse rushed in and said.

"I can't… I can't leave him here. He needs me. I… I need him," Ashanti sobbed.

"I understand ma'am, but you'll have to come back at the next visiting time," the nurse pleaded with Ashanti while looking at her with empathy.

"Ahmad please wake up… if you love me, wake up," Ashanti insisted as the nurse tried to pull her out of the room.

"I can't leave!! I just can't!" Ashanti screamed and pulled away from the nurse and ran back to Ahmad's side.

Another nurse, along with a security guard, barged into the room. Ashanti heard them as they called out to her and told her that she had to leave the room, but she ignored them. When one of them grabbed her, she screamed uncontrollably and struggled to get free from his hold. Ashanti stomped the security guard's foot and broke away from him when she saw Ahmad's eyes open.

"He's waking up! He's waking up! I told y'all he needed me!" Ashanti exclaimed with much happiness and relief.
***

Ahmad listened as everyone came in and visited with him. They all told him how much of a fighter he was, and they knew that he would pull through. He heard his homie and best friend Seth, his coach, his dad, and then Aaliyah. Ahmad was more than happy to have everyone check on him, but he couldn't help but to wonder where Ashanti was. He figured that she would be the first person to come and see him, but he was wrong.

A little while later, when the door opened, Ahmad felt Ashanti's presence and felt himself smiling, even though his face remained stoic on the outside. When Ashanti grabbed his hand, Ahmad tried with all of his might to squeeze back, to no avail. The moment he heard her voice, his heart began to smile.

"I can hear you baby. I'm not leaving you," Ahmad tried to say out loud, but his lips never moved.

Someone rushed into the room and tried to make Ashanti leave, but she stood her ground. Ahmad laid there fighting with all of his might to wake up. When a security guard rushed into the room, Ahmad finally blinked, and Ashanti saw him.

"He's waking up! He's waking up! I told y'all he needed me!" Ashanti exclaimed.

The nurses ran over to Ahmad when they saw that his eyes were really opened. One of them hit the button and called for the doctor. A few seconds later, all of Ahmad's medical team burst into the room and began checking his stats. The machines started beeping like crazy, and Ashanti screamed because she had no idea what was going on. One of the nurses asked her to leave and practically pushed her out and closed the door. She yelled and told Ahmad that she was right outside of the door and wasn't leaving.

Ahmad heard the doctor yelled out different things but didn't understand what the hell he was saying since he was talking so fast. Ahmad winced in pain and tried to sit up when he felt them hitting on him. .

"You feel all of that" the nurse asked him.

Ahmad shook his head *yes*, and they all cheered. It was then that he remembered them talking about the possibility of him being paralyzed. When he tried to speak, his throat was dry, and the words wouldn't come out with sound. One of the nurses handed him a few ice chips from a pitcher that was on the counter. Ahmad ate them and felt ten times better when they slid down his throat. Testing out his vocal cords again, Ahmad was able to speak his first words.

"I know y'all didn't think I was gon' die?" Ahmad joked and sat upright in his hospital bed.

"It was pretty scary, but we all knew you were a fighter," Dr. Brandon replied with much honesty and sincerity.

"I wouldn't have had to fight so much if the anesthesiologist would have listened to you right?" Ahmad inquired without any qualm. The look on everyone's faces told him that he was right about what actually happened.

"Get my girl and my family in here," Ahmad requested with as much calm as he could muster.

Chapter Five

"Mommy, why everybody got a daddy except me? Where my daddy at?" Kya asked her mom one Friday evening after school. All of the kids in her first grade class were asked to bring pictures of their parents, but she noticed that she was the only one in her class at the time who only had one picture.

"You don't need a daddy. I got you," her mom replied to her.

"But... but I want a daddy too. You only gave me a picture of you to take to school," Kya sadly admitted.

"I'm gonna show you a picture, but if you ever see this man, don't say anything to him unless he speaks to you. Okay?" her mom iterated.

Kya wiped her tears away and began smiling from ear to ear. When her mom showed her the picture, she stared at it until her mom took it away. Kya watched as her mom put the picture inside of a book and placed it in the top drawer on her nightstand. She made a mental note to look at the picture every chance she got, and that was exactly what she did. Every time her mom got in the shower or went to use the bathroom, Kya made her way to the night stand, pulled the picture out, and admired it.

A few years later while they were leaving Wal-Mart, eight year old inquisitive Kya walked away from her mom while she was grabbing some groceries. When she rounded the corner, she saw Ashanti McNeal, a little girl who was in the same grade as her, but she had a different teacher. Kya ran over to her and spoke to her. Her and Ashanti walked away and went and looked at some toys. About five minutes into their play time, a man called out to Ashanti.

"I gotta go, that's my daddy," Ashanti told Kya and ran off.

Kya walked around the corner in just enough time to see the man that Ashanti ran up to. She stared at him until he walked away. On her way back to find her mom, Kya knew that he was the man from the picture her mom kept hidden. She wanted to chase after him, but she remembered her mom saying that she could never say anything to him. The man didn't seem to notice her, but she knew exactly who he was right away.

On the way home, Kya was as quiet as a mouse. Her little mind wandered all over the place. She figured that if the man from *the picture was Ashanti's dad, then he must be her dad too. When they made it home, Kya broke her silence by asking her mom a question that made her mom spaz out.*

"Is Ashanti McNeal my sister?" Kya quietly asked.

"Kya Taylor!! Don't you EVER let those words come out of your mouth again! Do you understand me? That man will be dead soon with the life he lives any damn way so forget about him!!" her mom scolded her. Kya went to her room and cried herself to sleep.

A couple of years later, the man from the picture died just like her mom said. Kya remembered Ashanti missing a few days from school. It was then that her mom once again told her to never mention anything to Ashanti. She heard her mom on the phone talking to one of her friends and saying that Ashanti was better than Kya because Al never had the chance to get to know her because of the situation.

"Big Al!!!!" Kya jumped up and said after she broke herself from her reverie.

It was Sunday and Kya was off, so she was sitting at home doing some thinking. Kya had pushed *that* picture that she stared at during her childhood pretty much every day to the back of her mind. She stopped torturing herself with thinking about the dad that she never had. After reminiscing, she was confident that Big Al was the man in the picture, even though she hadn't seen him in over ten years. The last thing she knew about her dad was that he was dead, so rapid thoughts were running through her mind expeditiously. She couldn't figure out why her mom said that he was dead, and why Ashanti and her family said that he was dead, but he was in prison. *"Was that where my mom was going on those Saturdays?"* Kya asked herself as she thought about how her mom would disappear on some Saturdays and never say where she was going.

Kya's phone rang and jolted her from her thoughts. She noticed that it was her job calling, so she answered. It was one of the supervisors on the phone, and he said that someone had called in and wanted to know if she could cover the shift. Kya's plan for the day only included relaxing, but after the revelation she just had, she decided that she would take on the extra shift and confront Big Al if the opportunity presented itself. She actually told herself that she would make it happen no matter what.

When she ended the call, a thought to call her mom popped into her head, but Kya quickly dismissed it. That had always been a sore topic for her mom, so she felt like it would be best to approach it from a different angle. Looking at the wall clock, Kya saw that she had two hours to get ready and be at work. She sat there for a few more minutes and thought about Ashanti. Kya really missed the friendship that they once shared. But her jealously always got the best of her, and she didn't know how to control it. Ashanti got the dad that she never had, and even the man that Kya thought she always wanted. Kya remembered how Ashanti was never even checking for Kentay until he wore her down. Deep down, Kya always wanted him because of his street status. When Kya got up, she told herself that it was time to make everything right in some kind of way. She always wondered if Ashanti ever knew that they were sisters but ignored the fact the same as she had done throughout their childhood and adult years.

Kya made it to work a few minutes late, but she wasn't too bothered by it because in her eyes, she was only helping out. The process of getting in and out had become a whole lot easier as the months passed. Like always, Kya headed to the shift staff meeting, but along the way, she got an eerie feeling from one of the inmates. The way he stared at her caused her to shiver on the inside, which made her start to regret taking on the extra shift. It was one of the men who had tried to talk to Kya before, but she brushed him off. He was also one of the men who jumped Kentay. Kya nervously continued on her way, but not without watching her back.

Four hours into her shift, it was time for Kya's break. She was ecstatic because things had been crazy as hell since she arrived. All she wanted to do was go to the break room and chill out. However, when she rounded the corner and saw Big Al, she remembered the real reason that she agreed to take on the extra shift in the first place. Big Al paused his movements when he saw her approaching, and they locked bleary eyes with each other. Even though her mind was full of rambling thoughts, Kya couldn't get any words to come out of her mouth.

"You know don't you?" Big Al broke the awkward silence and asked.

When Kya didn't reply, he gestured for her to follow him, and she did without any hesitation. It was as if Big Al always had his way and no one questioned him. He led Kya to an office that belonged to one of the correctional officers and walked in like it was his. Big Al motioned for Kya to have a seat in one of the chairs, and she timidly complied.

"I knew it wouldn't be long before you figured everything out," Big Al declared as he sat down and rubbed his bald head.

"Why was she more important than me?" Kya anxiously inquired, wanting to know the answer to the question that has been burning inside of her for years.

"That was never the case. The situation we were in was complicated as fuck. I ain't gon sit in here and try to make your mama look bad or no shit like that. I should have taken matters into my own hands anyway... but just know that I didn't even know you was mine until I was locked up and received a letter with some important details and pictures. After I was sent away, I wouldn't take visits from anybody because I felt like less than a man for fucking up my family. Even behind bars, I know what's going on out there. But to keep everyone safe, there's certain shit that I just can't do," Big Al spoke and then took a deep breath before he continued.

"I've kept up with everyone, but like I said... I can't reach out. When you started working here, I started calculating the right time to have this conversation. After seeing the look on your face, I knew today was the day. I can't come down on you because of the choices you've made. Hell, I made some fucked up ones myself or else I wouldn't be up in this bitch. But baby girl, you still have time to turn shit around. The shit you and Shanti fell out about ain't even worth it," he admonished.

"Does she know you're still alive?" Kya finally found her voice and asked after carefully listening to his overdue confession.

"Nope! You're the only one on the outside who knows besides your mom and Tina," Big Al responded.

"My mom knows? Why did y'all keep this secret? I need to know what really happened," Kya scolded with hurt in her voice and confusion expressed on her face.

"Well... going into all of that would only make me relive some shit that I need to forget. Just know that your mom has tried to visit me often, but I don't accept any visitors. Hell, Tina wishes I was really dead. I've reached out to Ashanti by mail, maybe one day she will get one of my letters. When you turn twenty-five, you will receive a letter with instructions on a trust fund. So will Ashanti. I would love for y'all to hash your problems out, but it's on y'all. I know I ain't got room to make no demands," Big Al stated with a sincere gaze towards his daughter.

"So basically, I'm still in the dark about everything. You answered questions without truly giving me some real answers. But that's straight though. At least, you finally acknowledged me," she rambled with tears in her eyes. She couldn't believe that she's finally face to face with her dad but still feel so alone. In an instant, her mind reflected on her relationship with Ashanti. "Damn! I was so stupid for turning my back on Shanti. I know she hates me and now that I...," Kya started saying then cut her sentence off.

"Now that you're sleeping with her ex huh?" he finished her sentence for her. Kya looked up and was shocked that he knew what she had been doing.

"Don't look so surprised. That's an insult. If I know everything that's going on out there, you know I know what's happening in here. That young nigga has a good heart, but he needs another reality check," Big Al observed.

They talked for a little while longer, and when Kya looked at the time, she noticed that her break should have ended twenty minutes ago. Even though Big Al told her everything was all good, she knew that she needed to get back to work. They both walked out and headed in different directions. Kya was more confused than ever before and her mind seemed to be in outer space. She failed to pay attention to her surroundings for the first time during that shift and was snatched up by a gang of inmates as soon as she rounded the corner. Before she could scream, her mouth was covered up, and she was knocked out cold with a fire extinguisher.

Chapter Six

After being delayed by two weeks, it was finally time for Kentay to be released. He was pissed off because he felt like Courtney was playing games and stalling with the test results. It didn't help that he spent the last week in the hole because of a fight he had with some niggas that gang raped Kya. If it had not been for Big Al, he would have been facing some more time in prison. Kentay knew that the man didn't care shit about him, but he had no idea why he had saved his ass and took part of the rap for him for what he had done. He chunked it up to figuring he was one of those old cats who were sweet on young girls.

Kentay was ready to get the hell out of prison and to get things back popping, but he was conflicted for some strange reason. He heard that Kya was in a coma after her ordeal. Although he still had hopes of getting Ashanti back, he had some ties to Kya that he couldn't explain and didn't want to leave her alone. Since it was Kentay's last day, and he didn't want any problems whatsoever, he decided to stay in his cell to avoid the hating ass niggas who were lurking.

"Mills," Kentay heard one of the correctional officers called out to him.

"What the fuck is it now?" he mumbled to himself while shaking his head.

When the officer made it to his cell, he looked up but never replied.

"This way," the CO told him, and Kentay hesitantly got up.

He followed him down the hall and instantly knew where they were headed. While on the way, Kentay cussed Courtney's ass out in his head. They never gave him a specific time that he was leaving, so he hadn't made the call to Slick and that bothered him since he was so far away from home. Even though they told him he was leaving that day, he was also informed that it could possibly be the next day because that was just how shit went sometimes.

They made it to the nurse's door, and the officer opened it and motioned for Kentay to go in. Just as he figured, Courtney was sitting there.

"Have a seat Mr. Mills," she said after the door closed behind him.

"Why the fuck you keep playing games, Courtney?" Kentay blurted out with much venom.

"I'm not playing games. I'm trying to get you out of here. All you gotta do is cooperate," Courtney retorted with a hellish grin.

"You still on that bullshit I see," he said while shaking his head and biting the inside of his jaw.

"I fucked up Tay, but you aren't exactly a saint either so cut the bullshit," Courtney snidely remarked.

"I didn't lie on the fucking floor and kill a baby did I?" Kentay angrily spat and hit the table and caused Courtney to jump.

"Then yo ass left and never looked back," he continued.

"You told me I was dead to you! What was I supposed to do Tay?" Courtney heatedly countered.

"So why are you here now?" Tay sarcastically inquired.

"Because… I never stopped loving you… and I wanna be a family," Courtney quietly replied.

Kentay stood there and stared at the woman who had his heart years ago. When he heard her say those words, feelings that he thought were long gone began to resurface. All it took was for him to think about what she did to snap back to reality.

"Family? We could have been a family Courtney, but you threw it all away. Ain't no family now. You know what you did," he told her.

"It's not too late," she replied and stared at him with the puppy dog eyes that always made him give in to her pleas back in the day.

"You killed my seed Court… I can't see myself acting like that's okay. It will always be on my mind," Tay sincerely told her and sat down in the chair directly across from her.

Shortly afterwards, Kentay put his face in his palms and began rubbing his temples. A million and one thoughts were running through his mind. He thought about what life may have been like if Courtney would have kept their baby. Would he have still met Ashanti and pursued her? Kentay loved Ashanti and he still wanted her, but being in Courtney's presence had him questioning his entire life, and he didn't like second guessing himself about shit.

"What we had was in the past Courtney. We just need to leave it there. I got a life and you got a life… let's not even fuck shit up," Kentay told her.

Courtney didn't reply, she just slid her phone across the table. Kentay was hesitant to pick it up, but went ahead anyways. When he finally looked closely at the phone, his eyes bucked like a deer caught in headlights.

"What the fuck? How…? What…? Who…?" Tay quizzically inquired as he stared at a little boy that looked just like a younger version of him.

"Don't just sit there looking crazy… what the fuck is going on?" Tay continued with shock and surprise written all over his face.

Courtney sighed and then began talking.

"I thought I lost the baby, but I didn't. I had no idea I was still pregnant until I gave birth a month and a half early. I wanted to reach out to you a million different times, but your last words to me always rang in my head and stopped me. I can't blame you for anything, but I moved down here to get away from everybody and everything. Imagine my surprise when I saw your name on the inmate list. Honestly, I never thought that I would see you again. After seeing you for these past few months and going home to my son, to our son and looking at a mini you, I knew that I had to tell you about him," Courtney stated in earnest.

Kentay sat there speechless. He really didn't know what the fuck to say. The information that Courtney had just dropped on him was unbelievable to him. Looking at the picture over and over again, he knew that the little boy had to be his child. How the hell it happened, he wasn't sure about, but he planned on getting to the bottom of it.

"Please don't be mad Tay. You just don't know everything that I been through or the shit I'm going through," Courtney sadly remarked.

"This shit ain't easy to process Courtney! You can't just drop this on me and think everything gon' be all good. It ain't like this a fuckin' new born baby we talking 'bout. You disappeared and now you telling me I got a son that's what? Six years old?" Kentay fumed.

"I can't deal with this shit right now!" he stated and got up and left.

He heard Courtney as she called out to him but continued walking. The bomb that she had just dropped on had him fucked up in the head. Kentay walked straight back to his cell. It was dinner time, but he didn't plan on eating another meal in that place. He sat down on his bed and thought about his baby with Ashanti who had died and thought about his daughter Kendra, whose life he was missing out on. Now, he had a six years old son, whom he had never even met, and he became very overwhelmed. Kentay was so used to being in control of everything, but his current predicament left him no choice in the matter, which caused him to re-evaluate some shit.

About an hour later, Kentay's roommate Scott walked in grinning.

"Why you looking so lost man? I heard you bout to exit this bitch!" Scott chided.

"Got a lot on the brain, but I'm damn shol' ready to dip out this mu'fucka man," Tay replied.

"Well, here come the people so get ready. Lemme get them phones up off ya tho," Scott stated in a hurried voice.

"Man, if they tell me I'm 'bout to go, you can have 'em bitches. My real shit at the house anyway. This half ass smart phone," Tay responded with a half chuckle.

A few minutes later, Tay looked up as his name was called. He knew that the moment had finally arrived when he looked up and saw the mean mugs from the guard who couldn't stand his ass.

"Let's go Mills," the other guard stated with much frustration. Kentay jumped up with the quickness. He didn't want any of the shit that he had acquired while incarcerated, so he quickly made his way towards the door. He gave his roommate some dap and told him to stay up. Just as he promised, he motioned to where the phones and the rest of the shit he hustled were hidden to let him know that everything was good and then dipped out. Kentay was escorted to the front and through the gates. When he realized that he hadn't called anyone to pick him up, he asked about making a call. The guard who hated his guts told him to use the phones that he had while inside and turned to walk away.

"Fuck!" Kentay spat. He was in the middle of nowhere and didn't know any fucking body. When he took one step, a horn blared. He looked up in the direction of the horn and locked eyes with Courtney. Even though he was pissed off at her, he didn't have any other choice but to go and hop in the car with her.

Chapter Seven

It had been one week since the shooting at the park, and surprisingly things were pretty much back to normal. Ashanti tried her best to wait on Ahmad hand and foot, but he wouldn't allow her to do too much for him. What he had overcome was a miracle in their eyes, and they were grateful. School was back in session, and summer was slowly but surely about to turn into fall. Ashanti was taking eighteen hours her sophomore year and finally decided on Public Relations as a major. Since watching Ahmad play, she'd grown to love sports and researched different careers that would allow her to work in the sports field as well as make decent money. The options with that degree with a minor in communications were endless.

After class on Wednesday, Ashanti decided to head to Weir since she was off. She hadn't been down to visit with her mom in a week. Kendra was in Jackson with Dennis until the weekend. It was amazing how everyone had stepped up and started taking care of her without any complaints. Kentay hadn't called Ashanti's phone in a few weeks, and she was happy about that and had hopes that he had finally let go of what was already over in her eyes. Since he was sentenced to so many years, she knew that Kendra would never even know who he was. That was something she had thought about a few times, but taking Kendra to visit him in prison wasn't something that she wanted to bring up or do.

Forty-five minutes later, she was turning into her mom's driveway. Ashanti noticed that her mom's car wasn't there and wondered where she could be. It was almost five o'clock in the evening, so she figured that she would be home. Shanti got out and used her key to go inside. The first thing she did was go into the kitchen to see what kind of desserts her mom had because she loved to bake. Her eyes lit up and her mouth got moist when she spotted the caramel cake on the counter. Only one slice was gone so Ashanti knew that it was good and fresh. She grabbed a knife and a paper plate out of the cabinet and cut two slices. After she poured a glass of milk, she sat down and devoured both pieces in just a few minutes.

When she finished, she pulled her cell phone out and decided to call her mom to see where she was. Her mom answered on the second ring.

"Hey ma… you supposed to be at home by now, where you at?" Shanti asked her.

"I'm grown Shanti… where you at?" her mom countered.

"Well, I came to visit you but you ain't here," Shanti replied.

"You shoulda called first girl… I won't be back for a couple of hours," Tina told her.

"Ugh… guess I'll catch you another time," Shanti said.

Since her mom wasn't about to be home anytime soon, Ashanti decided to grab some more cake for her and Ahmad and then head back to Starkville. Before she left out of the kitchen, she saw a pair of her mom's earrings on one of the end tables in the living room and knew that wasn't normal, so she went and grabbed them to take them in her room and placed the earrings in her jewelry box. When she placed the earrings inside, the box moved a little and Ashanti saw a couple of letters under it. Curiosity got the best of her, so she picked them up.

"Mississippi State Penitentiary… Kentay's ass," Ashanti mumbled while shaking her head.
Ashanti was about to put the letter back until she saw that it was dated for the year before.

"What the hell? He wasn't down there then. Who is this from?" Shanti mumbled to herself as she opened the sealed letter. Without a return name listed, she had no idea who it was from and really wanted to know who could be writing her mom from prison. She began to read the letter.

Tina,

> *This is gon be short like always. Knowing your stubborn ass, you ain't even opened none of my letters yet. I'm giving it one more year before I reach out to Shanti on my own. This shit ain't even fair, and you know it. I can't bring your mom back, and I will hate that she was caught up in the crossfire of my bullshit until the day I die. I did what I had to do to make it up to you, and I can understand you hating me, but don't continue to let my daughter think I'm dead. That other situation, it was fucked up, but I can't change it. You have until one year from today to get back*

with me or I'm taking matters into my own hands. It's been almost a decade and enough is enough.
You might not love me, but I will love you always,
Big Al

Ashanti read the letter five times in a row without moving. She stood there frozen for about ten minutes until the house phone rang and snapped her out of her thoughts. Ashanti walked over and grabbed her mom's cordless phone from the nightstand and answered it. She said hello, but the only thing she heard from the other end was someone breathing. After no one said anything, Shanti hung up. When the phone rang again, she ignored it. Ashanti couldn't process anything. She wanted to call her mom, but what she had to say needed to be done face to face. Plus, she really had no idea how she would even handle the situation. She kept the letter and headed home.

Ashanti had no idea how she made it to her place, but when she focused and looked up, she was parked in her designated parking space. Ashanti made her way inside and realized that she had left the slices of cake on her mom's kitchen table once she walked into her own kitchen to grab a bottle of water out of the refrigerator. After she drank the water, Ashanti went and laid across her bed and read the letter a few more times. She pretty much had it memorized by now. Closing her eyes, Ashanti vividly recalled the conversation she had with her mom about the death of her daddy.

"Shanti baby... there's no easy way to say this... but your dad is gone, and he isn't coming back," Tina told Shanti one day after she came home from school.

"Gone where mommy?" Shanti quizzically inquired.

"He's just gone baby," her mom told her.

"Did he die like my teacher said her husband did and go to heaven?" Ashanti asked.

"You can say that because you won't ever see him again," Tina cautioned.

Ashanti began crying and her mom comforted her. A week later, they went to a funeral home and Tina told Ashanti to tell her daddy goodbye. They walked up to a casket, but it was closed.

"Can I see daddy?" Ashanti asked while tears ran carefree down her face.

"No baby. You just have to look at his pictures and remember him by them. He loves you, and he will always be in your heart," Tina replied. They left the funeral home, and Tina took Ashanti to McDonald's for ice cream and to play.

"Hey babe! What you thinking about? I been standing here for two whole minutes and you didn't even know," Ahmad stated as he made his way over to the bed where Ashanti was.

Ashanti couldn't find the words to reply, so instead of saying anything she just handed Ahmad the letter. She watched him as he read it and his mouth flew open.

"What in the hell? Does this mean? Is this from your dad? I thought you said... Wait a minute... I gotta read this again," Ahmad said with total amazement and wonderment.

"Yeah... it's from my dad. Imagine what I'm thinking. My mom has been lying to me for almost ten years about my dad being dead. And he's been in contact with her. You see the date on the letter? A year will be up next week," Shanti replied with total exhaustion as she sat up on the bed to face him.

"This shit is crazy. And yo, this the same prison Kentay at. You think they've met?" Ahmad inquired.

"I have no idea. I just don't know how to feel about all of this. How do I approach my mom because I accidentally found this letter? Do I just wait for another week and see if he reaches out to me? I'm so fucking confused," Ashanti admitted and flopped back onto the bed and put a pillow over her face.

"Babe... don't stress about this. Look at all this other shit we been faced with, and it all worked out. We will get through this too. I got you," Ahmad soothingly told her and laid on top of her and kissed her sweetly.

"Let me take your stress away babe," Ahmad whispered to her in between kisses.

Ashanti closed her eyes and moaned as Ahmad pulled her dress over her head, threw it on the floor, and then caressed her body with his tongue. With everything that had been going on, it had been a couple of weeks since they made love. Ashanti knew that drought was about to come to an end as she felt Ahmad lovingly move from her breasts down to her stomach, then thighs. He slid her thong to the side, and the next thing she felt was his tongue on her pearl. Ashanti quivered as he devoured her mound.

After two climaxes, Ashanti felt Ahmad as he entered into her wetness. She couldn't contain the sex cries that escaped her lips because he felt so good to her. Ashanti gyrated her hips and pulled Ahmad deeper into her after a few minutes of him sexing her.

"Ahhh… you feel so good baby," Shanti moaned and then pulled Ahmad's face to hers and kissed him passionately as she tasted herself on his tongue.

"You do too babe… shit! I'm 'bout to cum," Ahmad told her after he broke the kiss.

Like clockwork, Ashanti creamed on his dick as he came inside of her. When he fell down beside her and pulled her close, her phone rang with her mother's ringtone, and the problems that she had just forgotten about resurfaced in an instant.

Chapter Eight

Things had been crazy as hell for the past week in the streets, and all Slick wanted to do was find Buck and personally put a bullet in his dome for the bullshit he had done. That was much easier said than done because he couldn't find his ass anywhere no matter how hard he tried. Slick had everybody and their mama on the lookout, but the nigga was invisible. After putting everything together, he knew that it was Buck who shot up the park because he saw Slick's truck there. The people who reported back to Slick told him that the shots rang out right when Ahmad walked near the truck and that made Slick feel like he was slipping. He knew he fucked up by not making sure that Buck was at home when they blew his shit up, but he never expected him to retaliate so quick and in that manner. To make things even crazier, it appeared as if Kentay had fallen off of the face of the earth. The last time Slick talked to him, Tay had told him that it wouldn't be much longer and to be ready to drop everything and pick him up whenever. Every time Slick called the phone now, no one answered, which was why he and Dub were now on their way to the prison for the Saturday visit.

"That nigga probably done got into another fight and in the hole or some shit," Dub said.

"That could be true, but I'm getting a different vibe," Slick replied.

"But we bout to find out what the fuck is going on in just a minute," Slick continued as he turned onto the premises of the Mississippi State Penitentiary which was known as Parchman.

It was a few minutes before eleven in the morning when they arrived, so they sat in the car for a few minutes talking about business. Besides the issue with Buck, everything was going smooth. They both knew that the situation was a lot and needed to have been handled. Slick couldn't help but to blame himself for slipping a little because it wasn't like him to allow shit to linger on and not take care of business.

"Let's go in here and see what's up man," Slick said when it was about three minutes until eleven.

"Bet," Dub replied, and they both got out and made their way to the entrance.

Slick and Dub walked in, and the line was already long. They had been so engrossed in their conversation that they didn't even notice all of the people as they went inside. By the time they made it to the front of the line, it was almost 11:30. Slick grabbed the clipboard and looked for Kentay Mills' name, but he didn't see it.

"Can Kentay Mill's not have visitors today?" Slick agitatedly inquired.

"He could if he was here I suppose, unless he would've gotten into some more shit," the guard snidely replied.

"He gone?" Dub chimed in ad asked.

"Yep... next," the guard stated and motioned for Slick and Dub to get out of the way.

Both of them walked back out more confused than they were when they arrived. The way Slick clenched his jaws and balled up his fists, it was evident that he was frustrated and pissed the fuck off.

"Bruh... what in the entire fuck is going on? This nigga done got out and ain't said shit. What kinda bullshit is that?" Slick fumed.

"Something gotta be wrong, bruh. He gotta have a good explanation," Dub retorted as he opened the door and hopped into the passenger seat.

"Wait... ain't that Ashanti walking out? Look over there," Dub continued.

When Slick looked up, he turned his head towards where Dub was pointing, and sure enough, he laid eyes on Ashanti.

"Shanti!" Slick called out to her after he hopped out of the car and jogged towards her.

"Wassup baby girl... you came down to visit Tay?" Slick asked after he caught up to Shanti and hugged her.

"Hey Slick... hell naw I ain't come to see that asshole. I'm sure that's who you visiting though," Shanti rebuked.

"Well we were... but they said he got out," Slick told her.

"He got out? What do you mean he got out? He's supposed to have...you know what? Nevermind. He's not even my problem anymore. Still though... He got out and didn't tell you? He still on that bullshit I see," Shanti responded as she shook her head.

"Something ain't right. Ima get to the bottom of it though," Slick chided.

"Enough 'bout that. Now, on to you. Who the hell you visiting though if it ain't Tay?" Slick quizzically inquired.

He noticed Ashanti as her facial expression changed before she replied.

"Well… it's a long story, but he's on lock down and can't have any visitors anyway, so it don't even matter," Shanti replied and looked at a woman that was walking in their direction.

"Miss Taylor, how are you?" Ashanti asked Kya's mom when she got closer to them.

"Hey Ashanti… I'm okay. I was… I was just… I'm headed to see Kya at the hospital but just stopped by here hoping that he would see me today," Miss Taylor replied with some hesitation as she was caught off guard and was not expecting to see her there. .

"He who? Never mind, it ain't my business. What's wrong with Kya?" Shanti politely asked.

"She was gang raped here on the job, and she's in a coma," Miss Taylor responded nonchalantly as if she just announced that Starkville was getting a Krispy Kreme.

Slick and Ashanti gasped very loud at the same time after hearing the news.

"Oh my God… what hospital is she in?" Ashanti asked with a lot of concern. Slick could tell that she felt bad for Kya by the look on her face, even though they were on bad terms. Slick stood there taking in all of the information with a mind full of thoughts of his own. He wondered if that was where Kentay was and if he was the reason that Kya had been hurt. Even though Kya wasn't his girl, he still had love for her. He couldn't explain his love for her because it was complicated, but he always wanted the best for Kya. Her tragedy would explain the reason Amanda couldn't get in touch with her for over a week. After a few more minutes, all of them parted ways. Slick wondered who in the hell Ashanti and Miss Taylor was there to visit. He walked back to his car when he saw Ashanti hop into the truck with Ahmad. Slick felt a little bad, but was happy to see Ahmad out and about. He vowed to make shit right with what happened to him.

Chapter Nine

Ashanti hopped into Ahmad's truck with her emotions all over the place. It seemed as if it was one thing after another. She had decided to pop up and visit with her dad after she googled the number to the prison and called and retrieved visitation information. Her mom had been calling, but Ashanti wasn't up for talking to her yet. She let all of her calls go to voicemail, but she did text her and tell her that she was busy to keep her from popping up.

"What's going on? That was the dude Slick right?" Ahmad asked her.

"Yeah that was him. I'm starting to wonder what's NOT going on!" Shanti exclaimed and began rubbing her temples.

"Why they wouldn't let you see him?" Ahmad inquired as he pulled out of the prison's parking lot.

"Something about he's on lockdown, but you remember my old friend Kya right? Well, that was her mom that walked off and went the opposite way of us. I don't know who she was visiting or trying to visit, but she had this weird expression on her face... and she also told us that Kya got gang raped, and she's in a coma. I feel so bad for her," Shanti emotionally explained everything to Ahmad.

"Oh and check this out... Slick said that Tay is out of prison. He was here to visit and found out he was already gone," Shanti continued her confession of surprising and upsetting news.

"What the hell? He got out and didn't call his boy? His right hand man?" Ahmad asked as he stopped at a red light.

"Same thing I said," Shanti replied melancholy.

"I hope he learned a lesson during his short stay," Ahmad remarked as he reflected on this unsettling news about his half brother.

"I won't hold my breath, but I hope so too for the sake of his child," Shanti stated with honesty.

"I'm probably crazy, but I'm feeling some type of way about the stuff with Miss Taylor. I know I haven't talked to Kya in months, but I feel like I need to see her," Ashanti said as she thought about the current state of duress her former best friend was in.

"We can go by there to see her. What hospital is she at?" Ahmad asked with sincerity.

"Her mom said she's at Delta Regional Medical Center," Shanti replied as she gushed out a deep sigh.

"I'll take you to see her, okay babe?" he responded. Ashanti nodded her head yes to answer him.

Ashanti plugged the hospital into her Google maps, and the directions popped up. It wasn't out of the way at all, and Ashanti felt like she was doing the right thing by going to visit. She knew that she was pretty hard on Kya when she wasn't there for her in her time of need, so she felt like the least she could do was not be a hypocrite and check on her. Ashanti started thinking about her dad again during the ride. She really needed to see him or at least hear his voice, so that she would know that he was really alive. She still hadn't figured out a way to address her mom. If her dad was alive, she didn't know what excuse her mom could possibly have to make her forgive her for all of the years she had caused her to miss out on. Why was he even in prison? This was yet another mystery to solve. She was just ready to receive some answers to the million and one questions she had.

Ahmad pulled up to the hospital thirty minutes later and parked in the first empty parking space that he saw. For some reason, a nervous feeling came over Ashanti, and she prayed that she was doing the right thing. They got out of the truck and headed towards the entrance. When they walked in, Ashanti walked to the receptionist and gave her Kya Taylor's name. She found out that she was actually on the first floor. Ahmad offered to go in and be with her for moral support. However, Ashanti thanked him but declined his offer by telling him that she felt like she needed to go alone. After she gave him a kiss on his sexy lips, she headed towards room number 115 and prayed every step of the way.

When Ashanti made it to the door, she knocked lightly, but no one answered. It hit her that Miss Taylor said that Kya was in a coma, so she eased the door open and walked in slowly and quietly. Tears streamed down Ashanti's face when she laid eyes on Kya's lifeless looking body. To see her so helpless tugged at Ashanti's heart, and she couldn't help but to feel sorry for her. Kya was bandaged damn near from head to toe, and it reminded Ashanti of one of those mummy people in the movies. She slowly walked closer to the bed and got a better look at the bruises that were on Kya's face. She was literally black and blue. Seeing her in such bad shape made Ashanti feel worse for how easy she had shut her out. She started thinking that she had turned her back on Kya and caused her to stray away further. In her mind, she knew that Kya was the type who needed guidance, but being in her feelings had made her selfish for one of the first times in her life.

"Hi Kya! I know we haven't talked in months, but your mom told me what happened, and I had to come and check on you. I really hate to see you like this, and I pray to God that you will pull through," Ashanti stated and then paused to gather her thoughts before she continued.

"Although I was pissed because you weren't there for me, I do realize that I never even gave you the chance to defend yourself. I apologize, and I do forgive you for everything. I know we won't be like we were before, but I do want you to get better so that we can hang out from time to time," Shanti sincerely stated.

Ashanti stayed and visited with Kya for about ten more minutes. She felt like it would be good to talk about some of the crazy things they had done in the past to lighten the damper mood. She laughed as she talked about the one time they had gotten caught pulling a prank on their English teacher by putting super glue in his hat and also in his eye drops. They had actually shared more good moments than bad. Before leaving her bedside, Ashanti said a prayer that Kya would pull through so that they would be able to make more memories. It was crazy to Ashanti how she instantly felt guilty about everything after seeing Kya in this restricted position. She wondered if it was God's way of bringing them back together as she left.

On the way out, Ashanti walked back to the lobby of the hospital in a daze. To see Kya so beat up and unconscious had really put her in a bad head space. When she rounded the corner, she saw Ahmad sitting in a chair in the corner watching TV. Out of her peripheral, she saw a guy smoothly approaching, but when she turned around, he was gone. To her, he looked like Kentay, but she shrugged it off and made her way over to Ahmad so that they could leave. She was ready to get away from the Delta and to head home and tackle another issue, her mom.

Later on that night, Ashanti was laying on the couch watching TV when there was a knock at the door. When they left the hospital earlier that day, she had plans on stopping in Weir to talk to her mom, but changed her mind once they made it to Winona. Ahmad tried to persuade her to get it over with, but her stubbornness shut him down at each of his approaches. Ahmad was at the gym with Seth, Aaliyah was with her mom, and Kendra was in Jackson with Dennis, so Ashanti had no idea who could be at the door. She slowly got up and made her way to the door and looked out of the peephole and saw her mom.

"Why didn't you use your key?" Ashanti asked when she opened the door wide to let her mom in.

"Well, I wasn't sure if I was welcomed or not, being as though you've been ignoring me for the past few days," Tina sarcastically replied.

"Please believe me, it was for the best," Ashanti mumbled and laid back down on the couch and started back watching TV.

"Shanti, you better tell me what's going on before I fuck you up for this shitty ass attitude you got," Tina scolded because she was tired of the lack of communication between her and her only daughter.

Ashanti continued to ignore her mom. Part of her wanted to know the truth, but the other part hated that she even picked up that letter and read its contents. She loved her mom dearly, but to know that she could have possibly been living one of the biggest lies ever had Ashanti feeling some type of way.

"Talk Ashanti Danielle McNeal!!" Tina exclaimed as she walked over to the TV and turned it off.

"Okay mom... have you really been lying to me for the last nine years, almost ten, about my dad?" Ashanti asked her as she waited for her mom's reaction.

She saw the shocked expression on her mom's face and instantly knew that her dad was really alive. Ashanti's stomach was in knots as she watched her mom walk away from the TV and flop down onto the love seat.

"Mom?" Ashanti pleaded, but Tina was unable to answer right then. Tina's reactions appeared like she had been sucker punched in the stomach as she was bent over and rubbed her stomach. Now that Pandora's box was opened, Ashanti wanted to know the truth and continued to push the issue.

"So it's really true? How could you lie about something like that mom?" Shanti asked as tears streamed down her face. She wanted to get away from her mom with the quickness, but she just couldn't move. Deep down Ashanti already knew the truth, but held out a little hope that everything might just be a nightmare and her mom would confirm it. Things didn't turn out that way though.

"Shanti... you don't know everything," her mom quietly stated.

"Tell me then, mom. Tell me what it is that I don't know so I can fill in the gaps... because right now, I do know that my dad is down in the Delta at the Mississippi State Penitentiary when I've been thinking that he was dead for almost half of my life. Is that why you never told me what cemetery he was in? Because he was never in one? How could you do that to me mom?" Shanti vented through tears.

"That man destroyed our family Shanti! I lied because I was hurt," her mom said as she cried herself. Ashanti wasn't used to seeing her mom cry, so she knew that something was terribly wrong. As she thought about it, her mom never even cried at the so called funeral for her dad.

"It's complicated Shanti, but I owe you an explanation now that you've found out. How did you find out anyway?" Tina asked after she wiped her tears away.

"That doesn't matter, mom," Shanti replied after she got up and started pacing the floor. She heard her mom let out a long sigh before she started talking.

"The real reason that I never cared for Kentay wasn't only because he was a dog, but he was also in the streets. And when you get involved with a man in the streets, you're always in danger. Your dad was a major player in the streets, and I didn't find out until it was too late. Everything happened so fast. One day, he came home and told me that he thought he had a child. But, he never said who it was by, and I never asked. All I did was pack my bags, along with your stuff and left. Me leaving that day turned out to be the worst thing that I could do because someone was after him. Since they couldn't get to him, they followed my every move. I told you that we were going to stay with gram and pops for a little while, and you were excited because they both had you spoiled rotten," Tina spoke as her tears started to flow again.

Ashanti started thinking about her grandparents and got sad as her mom talked. She really missed them. They had a double funeral, and both were closed casket, which made Ashanti feel like her dad's funeral was really legit.

"We had only been with them two days before they were taken away from us. Dad needed to run to the store to get his favorite ice cream for after dinner, and mom hopped in the car with him. You were on your way to get in the car too, but I made you stay because you hadn't finished your homework. The only thing you knew was that gram and pops had a car accident but that wasn't the whole truth. What you didn't know was that it was supposed to be me that got blown away. A timer and bomb was placed in my car. As soon as dad stopped at the stop sign, the car exploded. They were trapped and burnt to pieces. It was all because of your dad and his ego. Al tracked down the men and killed both of them with his bare hands, and then he went after their families and killed them too. One was a cop, and that's why he's in jail for life. It was easier to say he was dead and forget about him than to visit and relive that pain every single time I saw him," Tina continued talking. By this time, Ashanti had made her way over to her mom and wrapped her hands around her. They cried together. Ashanti wanted to ask some questions, but the only thing that came out of her mouth were sobs.

"I'm so sorry mom," Shanti finally managed to get out.

"You don't have anything to be sorry for. I know that it was wrong to do such a horrible thing, but once I did it… it was just easier to keep the lie going," Tina sighed and stated.

"I just don't know how to feel right now… about anything," Ashanti said after she stood up and started back pacing the floor.

"Did you ever find out if dad actually had another baby and who it was by?" Ashanti asked after several minutes of silence.

She watched her mom as she shifted in the chair. Her gut was telling her that some more shocking news was on the way, so she tried to prepare herself for it. Ashanti's palms got sweaty as she watched her mom, who was in deep thought. Her mom closed her eyes and rubbed her temples before she spoke another word almost five minutes later.

"Well… I put two and two together a few years back when I actually drove down to the prison to visit your dad. I never went inside when I saw her walk out. We were never friends or anything, but I did see her from time to time. And in my heart, I knew that she could only be there to see one person," Tina adamantly stated.

"Who? Who is the woman? Who is the child?" Ashanti nervously inquired.

"Kya Baby! Kya Taylor… is your sister," Tina stated with anguish as Ashanti's mouth flew wide open.

Chapter Ten

Kentay couldn't believe that he had been out of jail for a week and hadn't been home yet. He hadn't called Slick, Dub, or anybody, and he knew that he was tripping big time. He would have blown a gasket if the tables were turned, so he knew that he had to get his shit together and get it together as soon as possible. When he left prison a week ago, Courtney took him to get something to eat, and they talked some more in detail about shit that had gone on in their past. During their talk, Kentay held onto a lot of anger, but he admitted that he felt a little different after listening to Courtney's point of view without all of the fussing and cussing. In his mind, he had always told himself that he would choke the shit out of her if he ever laid eyes on her again, but deep down Kentay knew that he still loved her.

Kentay was conflicted about meeting her son, correction… his son. He knew that he needed to lay eyes on him to see if he felt a connection with the child instead of looking only at a picture. He didn't think that it would be wise to go with Courtney to her house. However, he really didn't have much of a choice in the matter since he didn't have his phone or his own ride. He devoured the food from the restaurant that they ate at. The prison food was definitely one thing that he knew he wouldn't miss.

Afterwards, Kentay rode in silence with his thoughts running wild as Courtney drove to pick up her son from the babysitter. On the ride there, it dawned on Kentay that he never asked for the child's name. When Courtney told him that she named her son Kentay Junior, Kentay dropped his head as he thought about the baby him and Ashanti had lost. After Courtney noticed his mood, she informed him that she was only joking and that his name was Kendall. As soon as Kentay laid eyes on him, his feelings were confirmed. They stared at each other for about five minutes before either of them made a move. Ever since that day, they had been bonding and making up for lost time. It wasn't his intentions, but he had made up for lost time with Courtney as well. It's the reason why he hadn't been able to leave until a week later after he talked her into letting him use her other car to go home and check on shit.

Kentay decided that he would head home around eleven o'clock Saturday morning. Courtesy of Courtney, he threw on some Jordan shorts, a tee shirt, and some slide in flip flops and headed out. On his way, he thought about Kya and felt bad about not checking on her. He knew what hospital she was in, so he decided that he would stop by. Kentay turned into Delta Regional Medical Center and parked on the side, so that he could gather his thoughts before going inside. Thoughts of being a better man for Kendra and Kendall were heavy on Kentay's mind. He knew that he hadn't been the best person at all, and he hadn't been a father at all, so he prayed that he would be able to get it right in the future.

After a few minutes of sitting outside, Kentay finally got out and went inside. Instead of walking through the front entrance, Tay ran and caught the side door when he saw a lady walk out. He made his way down the hall and started looking at the patient's names beside the doors. The hospital only had a couple of floors, so he figured it wouldn't hurt him to look on every door before he found Kya's name. Kentay saw the entrance to the front of the hospital but bypassed it and kept walking. He never saw Ashanti because he was looking one way. He finally found Kya's name and eased the door open and proceeded inside.

Kentay's knees buckled when he saw Kya. Although he knew that she had been hurt pretty bad, which was why he retaliated, the shape that she was in took him by surprise. He made his way up to the bed and looked down on her. The machines were humming, and Kentay found himself praying for Kya as he reached out and grabbed her hand. Normally, he wouldn't give two fucks about a female other than Ashanti. But, he was starting to be more open and told himself that he had to be a better person. He even wanted to be a better guy. Kentay visited with Kya for about fifteen minutes before he couldn't take anymore and left. On the way out, he met a nurse as she walked in. He could tell that she wanted to say something indicated by her facial expression. Instead, he spoke, kept going, and told himself that he would be sure to check back on Kya the next week.

Kentay made it to Starkville a little after two o'clock. The first stop he made was to Slick's crib. He had no idea if he would catch him there or not, but it was worth a try to make that his first stop instead of going to all the way to his house. Tay got out of the car and walked up to Slick's door. Before he could knock, the door opened, and he was faced with a death stare from his boy.

"Well, I would be happy to see yo ass, but being as though you been out a whole got damn week, I don't know how to feel," Slick vented before Kentay could say a word.

"You got every right to be pissed off… I swear you do, but Ima explain everything to you bruh," Tay replied. He couldn't even be mad or give Slick an attitude back because he knew his boy always meant well.

"You got a helluva lot of explaining to do man. Me and Dub drove down there to visit only to find out yo ass was out. That was beyond fucked up man," Slick hissed.

"Courtney!" was all Kentay had to say for Slick to change his demeanor.

"Oh shit! Where the fuck you see her at? Did you kill her? Come on let's go inside," Slick said and finally let Kentay in.

Kentay walked in and sat down on the couch. He watched Slick as he walked to his bar and grabbed a new bottle of Hennessy. Tay took the double shot that his boy poured for him and downed it before Slick even sat down. Kentay grabbed the bottle that Slick placed on the table and poured himself another drink. He decided to drink it slow as he told the story. By the time he finished running everything down almost an hour later, Slick wasn't pissed off at him anymore. After all of that was squared away, it was Kentay's turn to listen to everything that had gone down on the streets. He was pissed the fuck off to find out that it was his cousin who had shot his brother. It was still strange for him to actually call Ahmad his brother, especially since he now had his girl, but it was the truth. Kentay sat there plotting as he listened to Slick. He didn't know exactly how he was about to execute things, but he knew that some shit was about to go down very soon.

Chapter Eleven

"No... stop... what are you doi...?" Kya screamed before her mouth was covered and the beating began. She couldn't tell how many people were torturing her, but she knew there were at least four sets of hands that were on different parts of her body as they ripped her clothes off and beat her until she passed out. She heard everything around her until a forceful blow to the head turned everything jet black.

Kya had no idea how much time had passed, but she sensed that she was in the hospital by the beeping noises and the voices of doctors, nurses, and her mom in the room very often. One day, she even heard Ashanti and tried her best to wake up, but she just couldn't no matter how hard she tried. She wasn't sure if it was the same day or not, but Amanda had been to visit and she even heard Kentay say a few words to her. While being out of it, Kya had a chance to really reflect on everything that had gone on in her life, and she prayed to God for him to give her another chance to get it right. The fresh start to the Delta was supposed to be it, but once again she had made a terrible choice by sleeping with Kentay.

"God, if you give me one more chance, I promise to do right. I know I'm not perfect, but I will try my best. I miss my friend," Kya silently spoke to God.

When the room door opened, Kya tried to open her eyes, but she just knew that it would be the same as all of the other times. To her surprise, she saw light. As soon as she did, the machines started to go crazy, which caused Kya to panic.

"You're awake... calm down dear," the nurse spoke to Kya and then called for the doctor to come in.

The medical staffed rushed into the room, and Kya heard her mom in the hallway as she screamed and tried to figure out what was going on with her daughter. They made her wait in the hall, and Kya heard a nurse tell her that everything would be fine. She silently prayed that the nurse was right, but she wasn't so sure because she saw black once again. As hard as she fought against it, her body eventually succumbed to it.

About twenty minutes later, Kya opened her eyes again, and her mom was standing on the left side of her bed holding her hand.

"You scared the hell out of me these past two weeks. Oh my God... I thought God was going to punish me by taking you away from me," her mom cried as tears streamed down her cheeks. Kya opened her mouth to talk, but her throat was extremely dry, and it hurt too much to speak.

"Don't try to talk yet, the doctor said to give you a few ice chips first," her mom remarked and grabbed the cup from the tray and put a few in Kya's mouth. The ice felt like heaven when it hit Kya's mouth. Her mom gave her a cup full of ice chips and talked about all of the wrong things that she had done, which included not being there for her daughter in some of the most important times. Kya had never seen her mom so vulnerable in years, and she couldn't fault her because she was feeling the exact same way. When she tried to move, some pain shot through her body that caused her to wince and immediately stop moving. Without even seeing herself, she knew and felt that her body was severely damaged. Flashbacks of what happened popped into Kya's mind. Before she could stop herself, she was crying uncontrollably through the pain.

A nurse came through the door after the heart monitor they had on Kya continued to beep. She talked sweetly to Kya and told her that everything seemed bad for the moment, but she assured her that everything would be okay. She told her how her mom had been there with her the entire time, and she also described a few other visitors. Kya knew that she was talking about Amanda, Ashanti, and Kentay by the descriptions she gave her. When the nurse pointed to a table in the far left corner, Kya slowly moved her head that way and noticed the abundance of flowers, balloons, candy, and cards filled that side of the room. She was filled with so much joy. Out of all of the visitors that she had, she was the happiest about Ashanti. She knew that Amanda would be there for her regardless. However, she was shocked that Kentay stopped by, but to have Ashanti visit her in her time of need meant so much to Kya.

Kya asked to sit up. Just as the nurse and her mom were helping her up, the door swung open and in walked Amanda with more balloons and candy.

"Oh my gawwddd!! You're awake!!" Amanda beamed and her walk towards Kya turned into a jog as she made her way over to the bed and gave her a hug. Kya didn't feel any pain at the moment because the nurse had just given her some more pain medication.

"You had me scared shitless!!" Amanda practically screamed and then apologized to Kya's mom after she let her go.

"It's okay dear. I know you've been worried about your friend here. I'm just so thankful that she's awake," Ms. Taylor responded.

"Me too... thank you for being here for me," Kya said to her friend.

"Girl stop with the foolishness. You know I wouldn't have it any other way," Amanda told her. They talked for about an hour until Kya got another dose of pain medication. Her nurse told her that she would have to receive some intense therapy before she could even think about leaving so she needed to get her rest. Kya drifted back off to sleep but not before telling herself that she would call Ashanti soon and thank her for checking on her. She also had to officially break things off with Kentay.

Chapter Twelve

After Tina left Ashanti's place, she felt drained. The possibility of Ashanti finding out her secret had never ever crossed her mind. As she drove home, she deeply regretted the way that she had handled things. Even though Ashanti tried to act like everything was okay, Tina knew her daughter better than that. She knew that Ashanti was hurt and pissed off, and rightfully, she couldn't blame her. It wasn't in her character to be disrespectful, but the two times that she had slipped up, let Tina know that she was hurting. Tina knew that she had to do everything in power to make things right. There was only one way to start, and the next morning she was going to do just that.

Bright and early the next morning, after tossing and turning all night long, Tina got up and prepared herself to do something that she vowed to never do. By eight o'clock, she had showered, gotten dressed, made her daily cup of coffee and a small breakfast, and was out of the door. Since it was Sunday and she was going to miss church, Tina listened to gospel music for the entire two and a half, almost three hour drive. The invitation for her to visit was extended years ago, and it was made known that she was only one of two visitors that would be allowed. But, Tina never thought that she would actually follow through with visiting.

When Tina turned onto the grounds of the Mississippi State Penitentiary, her stomach dropped. The mere sight of the place disturbed her more than she thought it would. Just by looking at the outside, she could imagine that the inside was worse and not fit for a human being. Tina sat in her car for about twenty minutes before she finally got up enough nerve to get out. Tina sauntered inside and got in line. She was happy that the line wasn't long because had it been, she couldn't promise that she would wait and proceed with her plans. Five short minutes later, she was at the front of the line.

"Mrs. McNeal... what a surprise! I'm sure after being in the hole and just getting out late last night, your husband will be happy to know that you finally paid him a visit," the guard who had been working at the prison for over twenty years stated.

"I'm surprised myself, Joe," Tina replied as she made her way towards the direction that the guard pointed. Even though Tina had never visited or spoken with Al, she had Joe to keep her updated on how he was doing every step of the way.

Tina walked into the visitation room and took a seat at the table that was in the back right corner. She sat there for what seemed like an eternity, but in reality, it was only five or ten minutes before she spotted her husband walk through the doors. He looked even better than he did the last time that she had laid eyes on him. It was evident that he worked out religiously by the way his muscles protruded through his green and white jump suit. Tina couldn't stop the moistness that appeared between her legs. The man from church that was sexing her was nothing compared to her husband, and she instantly remembered everything that she had missed about him.

Instead of sitting down across from her, Big Al sat down right beside Tina and invaded her personal space. She inhaled his scent and knew that he had his favorite cologne, Giorgio Armani, on. Al was a man of power, so she knew that he had his way in and outside of prison. Tina's body shivered when Al placed his left hand on her right thigh.

"I can't believe your stubborn ass waited almost ten got damn years before you finally came to see me. What happened? Shanti found the letters?" Al stated while staring at her.

Tina was too caught up in the feelings that came rushing back to even reply at the moment. She sat there feeling worse than she did before she arrived for being so selfish. Al had been nothing but good to her, and she turned her back on him when he needed her the absolute most. She didn't know if she would ever be able to forgive herself.

"Don't sit here and beat yourself up now. I forgave you a long time ago, and I hope you've forgiven me by now. Just tell me what happened," he told her. Tina leaned over and hugged her husband, and she couldn't stop her tears from flowing. He held her tight as she got it all out and apologized to him over and over again.

Once Tina finally gathered herself, she told Al about the talk that she had with Ashanti and explained in detail what went down all of those years ago. Tina knew that if her husband had wanted to, he could have reached out to Ashanti in other ways. Instead, she respected the fact that he waited on her to make amends on her own time. She knew that he still felt guilty about what happened to her parents, and she imagined that some parts of him really wished that he was dead. They talked and talked and when there was thirty minutes left in the visit, Al got up and led Tina towards a door in the back. She noticed all of the guards turned their heads away as she quietly followed her husband. He told her that the prison allowed conjugal visits, but they would waste ten minutes walking to the building. So instead, he took her to the place that he had envisioned for damn near ten years and gave her what she had been missing for the remainder of the visit.

All eyes were on Tina as she walked out, but she paid them all no mind. She left feeling refreshed with a smile on her face and wanted to sucker punch herself for being such a bitch for so long. When Tina made it outside, she practically skipped like a school girl on the way to her car.

"So he let you visit huh?" a voice said that caused her to stop in her tracks just as she reached her car.

Tina paused before she turned around to address the lingering situation that had been avoided for almost a decade.

"What did you expect, Sheila? Did you think he would turn me around like he's been doing you every week that you've driven down here and wasted gas?" Tina casually inquired.

The telling expression on Sheila's face revealed how shocked she was that Tina knew about her frequent and pointless visits to the prison.

"Didn't think I knew? You should've known better sweetheart," Tina emphasized. They stood there in a stare down for about three minutes before the silence was broken.

"You don't even want him," Sheila found her voice and retorted.

"Unlike most women, I never blamed you for the shit that went down between you and my husband, but don't get the shit twisted... I will still fuck you up. What and who I do or don't want isn't your concern. Al doesn't want you, so get over that fling of the past. To have a child and not tell him he was the father until years later is the only thing you need to worry about," Tina snidely remarked.

"To fake your husband's death and lie to your daughter is lower than low so don't try to come for me, Tina. Does Ashanti finally know the truth?" Sheila replied without backing down.

"Once again, you worried about shit that doesn't concern you. How about you be there for your daughter during her time of need instead of running behind a man for once in your life," Tina responded as she stepped towards Sheila and closed the gap that was lingering between them.

Before any other words could be spoken, Tina saw a few people walking towards their direction. She didn't want to cause a scene at the prison, so she stepped back. There was so much that she could have said and done but chose to take the high road since she knew deep down that she had made some terrible decisions. But, she would never give Sheila the satisfaction of knowing that anything she had said got to her. However, Tina knew just the thing to clap back at Shelia without even touching her and to rub in her irrelevance in Al's life.

"That dick that you been chasing all these years, hunny, I just got it good with no problem on my first visit after 10 years. Now, you can take your pathetic ass home since you'll never get that dick again," Tina taunted and hit the unlock button to her car doors and got in. She crunk up, put her shades on, placed the car in gear, and left Sheila standing there in the parking lot looking like a fool.

Chapter Thirteen

Ashanti didn't know what or how she was feeling or how she was really supposed to feel after she finished talking to her mom the night before. For the first time ever, Ashanti felt a feeling towards her mom that she had never felt before. She wasn't sure exactly how to describe it, but she knew it was more than anger because she felt betrayed. Although her mouth said that she was fine, her body language told a completely different story, and Ahmad picked up on it right away. When he made it back from the gym, Ashanti was laying across the bed crying. No matter how hard she tried to stop her tears, they just continued to stream down her face, causing her eyes to become puffy and red. Ashanti wasted no time filling Ahmad in on everything that had transpired. She learned that he was the one who had encouraged her mom to come up and visit. She couldn't be mad at him because she knew that he meant well and was only trying to help the situation.

As a distraction, Ashanti decided to get up early the next morning and cook breakfast for her and Ahmad. She washed her face, brushed her teeth, and then strolled into the kitchen. When she looked in the refrigerator, she noticed that there were only a couple slices of bacon in the pack. Ahmad loved Wright bacon, so she knew that she was going to have to run to Wal-Mart or Kroger real quick. Ashanti slipped on some black tights, a Mississippi State tee shirt, and her white converse, grabbed her purse, phone, truck keys, and headed out of the door. Ahmad was still sleeping, and she expected him to be out for at least another hour or so.

While riding down highway twelve, Ashanti noticed that the cops had a black on black Dodge Charger that was sitting on some twenty two's pulled over and blocked in. There were at least five cars, and she wondered what in the hell was going on at seven o'clock Sunday morning. She shrugged it off and proceeded on down the highway. Once she got to the light by Apple Bee's, instead of turning right heading to Kroger, she bypassed Kroger and went ahead to Wal-Mart since she needed to pick up some more Dove body wash.

Since it was early Sunday morning, Wal-Mart wasn't packed like it normally was, and Ashanti was ecstatic about that. She made a mental note of her list and knew that it would only take her about fifteen minutes max to pick up her items, even with only the one or two registers they would have open. Ashanti sauntered inside, grabbed a cart, and headed to pick up her body wash first. After picking up the Dove and a few other items, Ashanti decided to walk towards the back of the store and make a loop. As she rounded the automotive department, Ashanti's phone sounded, and she knew that it was a text from Aaliyah by the tone.

Aaliyah: *what the hell happened to you calling me back yesterday?*

Ashanti: *Girl... I gotta fill you in on some shit. We gotta link up today!*

"So... it was really that easy to just turn your back on me? After all we've been through together wife, you can turn your back on your husband without a second thought?" Ashanti heard that familiar voice and looked up from her phone and stared right into Kentay's face.

"Yeah... I know you shocked to see me. Answer the question though. I know I did a few fucked up things, but was it enough for you to just say *fuck me* in my time of need?" Kentay inquired.

"First of all, you got life messed up because I'm not your wife anymore," Ashanti snipped without returning any formal greetings. Noticing the confused look on his face, Ashanti went ahead and explained herself. "See, that was some backhanded shit that you did to me in Vegas Tay, and there was no way in hell that I was gonna stay married to you. Even though you refused to sign the papers, the judge granted my divorce after learning how we were married. So, I didn't need your signature after all. If you don't believe me, check with your damn lawyer," she blasted feeling herself becoming heated and upset. Ashanti took a deep breath to calm herself down, but this unexpected encounter had gotten under her skin more than she wanted to acknowledge. Now that she had calmed down, Ashanti continued to address the remaining part of his questions.

"Secondly... A few? A few Tay? You and I both know that is a damn lie. You fucked one of my friends and had a baby by her. I think that alone was enough to end this relationship, but my dumb ass didn't even end it right away. You might love me, but you're not in love with me, and I'm not in love with you anymore either. What we had wasn't that happily ever after type of love and that's what I have now. I hate that Ahmad ended up being your brother, but it is what it is. Had you made it known from the jump since you knew, it may not have happened. I'll never regret what we had because it taught me a lot, but it's over Tay. It seems like you would be asking about your child that WE are raising, but I see you still on the bullshit," Ashanti casually replied while her heart raced like Usain Bolt was its biggest competitor. She surprised him with her response judging by the expression on his face and his silence. Ashanti didn't have anything else to say, so she made her way around Kentay and headed towards the grocery section.

Before she could get away, Kentay lightly grabbed her arm. The way that she looked at him caused him to let her go immediately.

"My bad… I didn't mean nothing by it. You right Shanti. I did some fucked up shit, but I always thought that we would be able to work through anything. I can be a man and admit that I did take some shit for granted. I took you for granted, but that don't mean the love that I had for you wasn't real," Kentay honestly replied.

Ashanti sighed before she responded.

"Tay… in life we all have choices, and there are consequences to those choices. We both made some good and bad decisions, and we have to deal with them. I don't hate you, but the only thing we have to discuss is Kendra. When you're ready, call Ahmad," Shanti told him and walked away.

The possibility of seeing Kentay in Wal-Mart that morning never crossed Ashanti's mind. After she checked out and was on her way back to her apartment, she reflected on the conversation she had with him and was very proud of herself. She didn't yell, slap, or do anything crazy for all of the hurt that he had caused her. All she wanted was to be free from their relationship, and she could tell that her words were finally sinking in. Ashanti was shocked that Kentay didn't say or do more, and for that, she knew that something had happened that had matured him, whether it was prison or not.

When Ashanti made it back to her place, it was fifteen minutes after eight. She walked in and went to the kitchen to place the items down, and then went into her room and saw that Ahmad was still asleep. She placed the body wash in the bathroom and headed back to the kitchen to start on breakfast. Less than an hour later, she was almost done when Ahmad walked into the kitchen and hugged Ashanti from the back.

"Good morning, beautiful," he whispered into her ear and then nibbled on her neck.

"Good morning, handsome," Shanti replied and then turned around to face him and gave him a hug and a kiss.

Ahmad picked her up and placed her on the counter and kissed her as he fondled her breasts.

"You gon make me burn the food baby," Ashanti cooed as she playfully tried to get away from him.

"I guess I'll let you make it for now. You went out?" Ahmad asked as Ashanti noticed him looking at the bags.

"Yeah… we only had two slices of your favorite bacon, and I knew that wasn't gonna work. I gotta tell you who I ran into, but it can wait until I finish up," Shanti grinned.

"Don't tell me it's some more drama," Ahmad asked as he grabbed a piece of bacon and ate it while Ashanti's back was turned as she broke eggs.

"I hope not, but I'll tell you. I'm almost done," Shanti answered.

About ten minutes later, Ashanti had all of the food on the table. She called out to Ahmad, and he came within thirty seconds. She had prepared blueberry pancakes, sausage links, bacon, and scrambled eggs with cheese. They had orange juice to drink.

"Don't think I don't know you swiped a slice of bacon," Ashanti laughed after Ahmad said grace. He couldn't do anything but laugh because he was guilty.

Over breakfast, Ashanti filled Ahmad in on her encounter with Kentay. They discussed Kendra's needs and agreed to be mature adults and handle the situation accordingly. Ashanti told Ahmad that she planned on meeting up with Liyah later on while he admitted that he was going to watch football with the boys. After they were done eating, Ahmad helped Ashanti with the dishes where the topic of discussion shifted to her parents. Ashanti was still feeling lost about everything, but she knew that seeing her dad soon and very soon was a must. It was imperative.

Chapter Fourteen

Kentay noticed a nail in the tire, and it led him to Wal-Mart bright and early Sunday morning. He had been calling Ashanti nonstop in hopes that she would unblock him, but after he talked to her, he knew that it was out of the question. Kentay was battling with his feelings of walking away from Ashanti or fighting for her. Once she found out he had another child, Kentay figured his chances would really be shot to hell, but he still didn't want to give up. After she walked away from him, all the words that she had spoken rang loudly in Kentay's head as he stood there in shock. He made a mental note to call his lawyer for clarification on this divorce he knew nothing about. He reflected on how many times he tore up those damn divorce papers, but in the end, it didn't mean a damn thing. Ashanti was no longer his, even though his heart wasn't matching what his head was trying to convey. When he heard his name called over the intercom to come to automotive, he broke out of his trance and headed to pay for the repairs.

As soon as he hopped into the car, his phone rang. It was Courtney.

"What's up?" he said as soon as the call connected.

"Hey… I was just checking on ya," Courtney replied.

"I just had to get a tired fixed. A nail was in it, but other than that, I just been getting shit back in line. What's up wit' you?" Tay asked.

"Nothing much. Kendall asked about you yesterday," Courtney answered.

"Tell lil man I said what's up, and I'll see him soon. I just gotta get everything straight on this end first," Tay replied very candid.

"I'll tell him. I have an appointment tomorrow, so he will be with my friend after school. Be sure to let me know when you coming back this way," Courtney responded.

They talked for a few more minutes and then hung up. Kentay realized that Courtney was being so nice because she felt guilty for the shit that she had pulled by not letting him know that he had a son. He was going to be there for them, but he didn't want to just hop into a relationship with Courtney again. Although they had been having sex on the regular, Kentay still told her not to get caught in her feelings. He knew that it was easier said than done, but he needed to say it so he did. Before he could do anything, he needed to handle the problem that had been lingering on the streets. For Buck to play Kentay, he knew that his cousin thought that he wouldn't be getting out of prison anytime soon. And, Kentay wanted everyone to keep thinking that, which was the reason why he instructed Slick to keep his return a secret for the time being.

Kentay headed back to his house after he left Wal-Mart. He hadn't dug deep to find out where Ashanti had moved to yet, but he would in due time. The words she spoke about Kendra popped into his head, and he needed to check on her. However, his pride wouldn't let him call Ahmad at the moment, even though he already knew his phone number by heart. Tay went across the street to Waffle House and grabbed him a to-go order because there wasn't shit in his house to eat. When he got home, he demolished his All-Star breakfast before he called his dad for something he had never done before in his life. He needed Dennis' advice. The conversation was short because Dennis convinced him to come down and visit. Since Slick was taking care of everything around the way, Kentay decided to take his dad up on his offer.

A little after two o'clock in the evening, Kentay made it to Jackson and turned into his dad's driveway. He was tempted to call Ahmad while he was on the way, but he told himself that he would call later on that afternoon. Kentay parked, got out, and as he was headed for the front door, it opened. He was amazed and surprised as hell when he looked down and saw his baby girl holding his dad's hand. Kentay couldn't stop the smile that spread across his face. He had only spent a short period of time with her, but it was obvious that he loved her as an unexpected tear crept down his face. He didn't realize how much he loved her or missed her dearly until now. His walk turned into a slow jog until he reached the door, bent down, and picked her up. Kendra looked at him strangely, but she didn't cry. Kentay told himself that he definitely had to step up because it was evident that she didn't know who he was.

"It's good to see you, son. And that young one there is growing up so fast," Dennis stated, feeling very elated.

"Good to see you too, pops. I see she is. It feels like I missed out on so much. I had no idea you had her with you. I thought she was with Shanti and Ahmad," Tay remarked with total excitement.

"We have a pretty good system going with taking care of her, but she's no problem at all, so I kept her this weekend. I didn't tell you because I wanted it to be a surprise," Dennis happily responded.

"It's a great surprise. I wanted to talk to you about some stuff too. I know it's time for me to get my shit together. I got two kids to take care of," Kentay put it out there to get it off his chest.

"Two? What do you mean two? What are you saying son?" Dennis inquired.

"Yeah… it's a long story, and I'm 'bout to fill you in on it," Kentay told him.

"Well, let's go inside and get comfortable. I have another surprise for you later," Dennis replied and then ushered Kentay inside. He was still holding Kendra as she was drifting off to sleep.

While Kentay familiarized himself again with his daughter and doted on his sleeping beauty, Dennis went out and retrieved to-go plates from Golden Corral for them. Him and Kentay talked and ate for the next two hours. Kentay found it good to actually have a real one on one conversation about life and choices. Kendra finally woke up, and Kentay went and got her and fed her some mashed potatoes along with a small piece of hamburger steak. Hearing his phone ding, Kentay picked it up to see that Slick had sent him a text message informing him that plans were in motion for what they had discussed the day before. Kentay replied to the text by sending the one hundred emoji as confirmation that it was on.

Kentay heard a car pulling up outside, and he saw Dennis get up and go to the door. He hadn't mentioned having any company, and Kentay wondered if he needed to go ahead and prepare to leave. He was enjoying bonding with his daughter, but he didn't want to intrude on anything else. A few minutes later, Ahmad walked in the house followed by Ashanti. As soon as she saw them, Kendra hopped down out of Kentay's lap and ran towards the both of them smiling and giggling. Kentay watched as Ahmad lifted her up into the air and spun her around. Ashanti took her from him and loved on her for a few minutes, and Kentay finally heard Kendra speak a few words. His blood began to boil, but he didn't know if most of it was because of the interaction Kendra had with Ahmad and Ashanti or if it was seeing them together. He still mulled over the fact that Ashanti's words were true and that they were divorced. After their confrontation in Wal-Mart, Kentay had called his lawyer later that day, who confirmed that they were indeed divorce. His love for Ashanti and semi-hatred for Ahmad ran strong causing him to see red. Instead of speaking to the couple, Kentay got up to head towards the bathroom when Ahmad spoke.

"What's up, bruh?" Ahmad said offhanded.

Kentay stopped in his tracks and bit his bottom lip before he said anything.

"What's up?" he replied with intensity and looked Ahmad in the eyes. The entire room grew quiet. Even Kendra stopped laughing as if she knew that something was about to go down.

"Okay… let's get this shit over with now and put it behind us," Dennis chided and broke the silence.

"Pop pop said shit!" Kendra screeched and lightened the mood for everyone just a little.

"Pop pop said a bad word, but you can't say it, okay?" Ashanti said to Kendra.

"I sorry Tee Tee," Kendra said and wrapped her arms around Ashanti tighter.

"You two, come with me!" Dennis said as he pointed at both of his sons.

Kentay watched Ashanti as she went and sat down on the couch with Kendra and grabbed the remote. He finally made his way outside behind Dennis and Ahmad about a minute later. He had been telling himself that it was time to grow up, but when different opportunities arose he found it harder and harder to do the so called right thing.

"Both of y'all are headstrong young men. This situation is far from normal and basically fucked up, but we ain't got no choice but to pull together and make it work. I ain't about to sit here and speak on either of y'all behalf… that little girl in there doesn't have a mother or a grandmother, but she has a strong support system. And, you two WILL do what it takes to make it work. Got it! Now talk and fix this shit," Dennis said his peace and walked back in the house.

Kentay had visualized so many things that he wanted to do whenever the opportunity presented itself that him and Ahmad would be alone. He wanted to develop a relationship with him but told himself that it wasn't possible until he got his revenge on Ahmad for kicking his ass. As he stood there, his thoughts continued to run rapid. Kentay stared at him, and Ahmad stared back without an ounce of fear. Kentay knew that he was wrong for the way he handled things at his step mother's funeral, and in that instance, he decided to let everything go and move forward. He made a step forward and saw that Ahmad tighten his fists.

"Nah man... it's cool. We really gotta move forward. I apologize for everything, and Ima do my best to make it right," Kentay told him. He proceeded forward and pulled Ahmad in for a brotherly hug where they embraced for the first time ever.

Chapter Fifteen

Three Months Later…

After what seemed like an eternity, Kya was finally being discharged from the hospital. She had been transferred to the swing bed side a couple of months before her discharge, where she received extensive therapy as well as counseling for her accident. Her mom, along with Amanda had been back and forth with her pushing her to fight through. It surprised her that Slick even came one time. Kya could tell that Amanda and Slick really loved each other, and she was happy for them. Being in a relationship was the furthest thing from her mind, but she did have some relationships that she wanted to salvage.

Kya was back in her old bedroom at her mom's house, once again back at square one. Her mom had someone clean out her apartment and move everything into storage until she figured out her next move. Kya vowed not to become depressed and continue her therapy at Community Counseling Services, the local mental health facility. She was given a list of therapist to research and noticed one that was highly recommended by the name of Twyla Turner. Even though Ms. Turner worked mainly with children, she took on adult cases from time to time. Kya planned on reaching out to her within the next week.

As Kya laid on her bed, her mind began to wonder. Before she knew it, she picked up her phone and dialed a number that she would never forget. She had no idea if the number had been changed, but she did it before she lost her nerve.

"Hello," the caller answered.

Kya paused before she replied.

"Hey Shanti," she said into the phone.

"Kya… how are you?" Ashanti sincerely wondered.

"Well… I think I'll be better once I see you, and we can talk face to face," Kya responded in a nervous voice.

"Are you out of the hospital and everything? I called a couple of times, and no one ever answered the room number I visited," Ashanti told her.

"I remember you coming. Thank you so much for that. They moved me to a different room when it was time for therapy," Kya said.

"Ohhh okay, that makes sense. I ain't gonna lie and say this isn't awkward. I've heard and discovered a lot since then, but I agree with you that we do need to talk. Where are you? Or do you wanna meet somewhere?" Shanti inquired.

"I'm actually at my mom's. You wanna meet at Local Culture in about twenty minutes?" Kya asked remembering how much Ashanti loved that yogurt place. Ashanti agreed and Kya hung up and got up to prepare herself. She had on a Nike jogging suit already. It was one of the few comfortable outfits her mom bought her in preparation for discharge. Courtesy of her mom, Kya had some box braids that @hairbytrecie had traveled and did for her. It was November, but winter hadn't found its way to Mississippi yet, so Kya was okay with the jacket that came with her outfit. She was out of the door and on her way within ten minutes after telling her mom that she was fine for the one hundredth time.

When Kya made it to Local Culture, she found a park right beside the McAlister's call in order space and parked. She walked in, and Ashanti was already inside waiting. Kya didn't know why she was shocked because Ashanti was always a prompt person. Both of them made their way to the counter and started fixing their yogurt without saying a word. Once they paid and sat down, Kya finally broke the awkward silence.

"I'm so sorry Shanti... even since my last fuck up, I fucked up again, and I gotta get it off my chest," Kya said and started crying right away. Her emotions were all over the place, and it was hard for her to control them.

"Kya, I'm sorry too. Everything isn't your fault. I know that I was a bit harsh. When I saw you lying in that hospital bed so helpless and looking lifeless, it made me do some serious thinking about life and everything. I've had my faults as well as you. I really don't want to relive any of it, I just want us to move forward as best as we can... especially since... we're sisters," Ashanti stated with hesitation to gauge Kya's reaction to the news.

Kya gasped because she had no idea that Ashanti knew.

"You know about it? How?" Kya inquired as she took a bit of her yogurt.

"It's a lonngggg ass story, but yeah I know. I have to go and see him soon," Shanti replied as her eyes began to water.

For the next three hours, Kya and Ashanti talked about everything under the sun. They laughed, cried, laughed some more and continued their rotation time until it was ten o'clock and the shop was about to close. Kya felt like she had her old friend back, and she was going to do everything in her power to make their friendship last this time around. As they walked outside, she knew that there was one more thing she needed to tell Ashanti and knew that it could possibly be a deal breaker. However, she needed to get if off of her chest so there wouldn't be any more secrets between them if they wanted a fresh start as sisters.

"Shanti…umm… there's one more thing I have to tell you about what happened at the prison," Kya said with uneasiness when they walked outside.

"Oh-kkk! What is it?" Ashanti inquired.

"Well… I did something else stupid that you might not forgive me for," Kya hesitantly stated.

"It can't be worse than everything we've already been through," Ashanti stated and laughed in an attempt to break the tension that appeared.

"I slept with Kentay while I was working there," Kya finally blurted out.

Ashanti didn't say anything for a full sixty seconds, and Kya was nervous as hell. When Ashanti chuckled, she became confused.

"Kya… who he fucked or didn't fuck is no longer my concern. Kentay has no more control over my life. I honestly thought you fucked him a long time ago. If you want Tay, you can have him. I've moved on to much better," Ashanti adamantly stated causing Kya to sigh in relief.

"But if you even think about fucking Ahmad, I'll kill you," Shanti seriously warned her and smiled. After hearing that declaration, Kya hugged her and told her that she promised to be a better friend and sister and to put all of her foolish ways behind her. Before they parted ways, they promised to take things slow but stay in touch. Kya headed back home feeling refreshed and prayed that she would take this new chance at life and really make the best of it. As she traveled back home, Kya dialed Amanda's number, but she didn't answer, so Kya left her a message and told her to call her when she got a chance. Kya was elated that things were finally coming together for her.

Chapter Sixteen

After Ashanti's spur of the moment meeting with Kya, instead of heading home, she headed to Ahmad's apartment. They had pretty much been spending all of their time at her place, and she agreed to stay at his place for the night. When she left Local Culture, Ashanti had a million thoughts on her mind. It seemed like some new drama popped up every single day. The past three months had been crazy as hell. Surprisingly, Kentay had been cooperating with them with only minimal drama so they were thankful for that. Ashanti didn't see him often and that was alright with her. Since she knew him all too well, she concluded that he had something else going on. It wasn't her concern, so she just let it be. Ashanti loved Kendra like she was her very own. In a weird way, she finally came to terms that it may have been best that she lost her baby considering the current circumstances. It still made her sad from time to time, but she was dealing with it quite well.

On her route to Ahmad's place, Ashanti decided to call Liyah and tell her about what had just happened. Liyah had been her voice of reason so much lately. Ashanti knew that she would be happy to see that she was mature enough to forgive Kya after the things that had happened. Aaliyah was always a person who found the good in everything. She wasn't the jealous or clingy type of friend like they saw with a lot of females on campus. To get mad when your friend meets a new friend was insane to them, but they saw it happen daily. Ashanti could honestly say that she found her best friend in college and would forever be grateful for the first class they took together in Lee Hall.

They chatted until Ashanti turned into the Highlands and into Ahmad's driveway. The sight before her caused her to scream "What the fuck?" as she turned the truck off and hopped out without giving Aaliyah an official goodbye. She never heard Aaliyah asking what was going on.

"What the fuck is going on? Is this the same bitch from the store? Sabrina wasn't it?" Ashanti fumed as she approached Ahmad and the girl standing outside arguing.

"Who the fuck you calling a bitch? You hoe! Wasn't you just fucking with his brother?" Sabrina fired back.

Ashanti was ready to hit her in the mouth, but her eyes locked in on her stomach and took her breath away.

"It ain't even what you thinking baby!" Ahmad stepped in front of Ashanti after noticing the despondent expression on her face.

"Oh, so you saying I ain't pregnant wit' yo baby? You better tell this hoe the truth and send her back to ya big brother," Sabrina loudly stated.

"Pregnant or not, I'll whoop yo ass if you don't shut the fuck up!" Ashanti firmly said and tried to step around Ahmad, but he blocked her path.

"Nah… let me get to her since her mouth so fucking slick," Ashanti said through clenched teeth as she continued to try to get around Ahmad.

"Sabrina!! Cut the bullshit… you know it's no fucking way I could be the father of your child. I asked you to leave five minutes ago and you still here on some shit," Ahmad fumed in a menaced-laced voice.

"How it ain't no way? Like I wasn't laid up in your place and in your bed. You got pictures of your family in the living room and that king size bed in your room with them maroon thousand thread count sheets feel like heaven. You rotate between your Mississippi State bedding and the black and white quilt your mom made for you," Sabrina stated with a smirk on her face.

"Oh… and let's not forget about your birth mark that's right…" Sabrina continued until Ahmad cut her off.

"See, I knew you was one of them gold digging broads which is why I DIDN'T fuck with you… get away from here before I let Ashanti go and let her whoop yo ass because you know I ain't gon lay hands on you," Ahmad threatened .

"You know what… this ghetto bitch sure does know a lot. How about y'all work this shit out while I take my ass home," Shanti quipped as she tried to walk back to her truck. Ahmad's grip tightened around her, and she wasn't able to move an inch.

"Shanti… you not going anywhere so calm your little ass down," Ahmad adamantly stated. Ashanti heard the seriousness in his tone so she stopped fighting against him. They had been through a lot of shit, mostly on her behalf. So, she figured the least thing that she could do was wait and hear him out without the bitch being present.

"I'm going inside. Get rid of her right now!" Ashanti instructed. When she made a move towards the apartment, Ahmad let her go.

Ashanti casually walked away in an effort to act like she was unbothered on the outside, but on the inside, she was pissed the fuck off. Initially, when she pulled up, all Ashanti saw was a girl trying to hug Ahmad and him attempting to move her and her hands away from him. Later, after she hopped out of the truck and moved in closer to them, she overheard them arguing while his raised voice indicated that he was pissed. She knew that he was mad by the way his jaws clenched and by the way he pronounced every syllable in each word. He only did that when he was trying to keep his anger in check. When Ashanti identified the girl as the one who came to her job with Ahmad and then noticed that she was pregnant, an unfamiliar feeling slivered through her body that she couldn't explain. She recalled that her and Ahmad were in a rough patch during that time, but he told her that he never slept with the girl. But now, she popped up pregnant. Ashanti paced the floor nonstop until two minutes later when Ahmad walked in.

Before Ashanti could open her mouth to say anything, Ahmad made his assertion. "That's not my baby! I don't know what kinda games she playing, but I swear it's not my baby," he confessed as he walked up to her.

"Ahmad... we said that we would always be honest with each other. I know we've dealt with a lot of my bullshit, but I've always been straight up. If there's a chance that she's carrying your baby, tell me now. I know you kicked it with her and shit early in our relationship. We might not have even been official yet, but if you lie now and it ends up being your baby... I just don't know," Ashanti told him.

"Baby, listen to me. It's not my baby. I don't like you doubting me and shit, but I know this looks foul, but I never fucked that girl," he told her as he grabbed her hands.

"Okay... I don't want any bullshit from her ghetto ass later... I'm just confused as to why she would even make such allegations and y'all never had sex," Shanti replied.

"I was tryna figure that shit out too. But, the first woman and only woman that's gon have my baby is you," Ahmad said and pulled Ashanti in for a kiss.

Ashanti's body yielded to him instantly. She wrapped her arms around his body and passionately reciprocated kissing him back. Within a few moments, Ashanti had taken control of the kiss and pushed Ahmad down on the couch. She placed kisses on his lips, then removed his tee shirt and allowed her lips and tongue to meet his chest and rippled abs. The lower she traveled, the more Ahmad moaned, and it turned her on that much more. When Ashanti reached Ahmad's dick, it was hard as a rock, and she could see it standing at attention through his gym shorts. She tugged at his pants, and he rose up a little and allowed her to pull them completely down. Once her little slugger was free, she admired it before taking him into her mouth.

Ashanti rotated between licking, sucking, and deep throating Ahmad's shaft. She had become such a pro at giving head that when he fucked her mouth, she didn't even gag.

"Oooh baby... shit! That feel so good," Ahmad moaned as Ashanti continued to do her thing.

"You like that baby?" she teased when she finally gave his dick a break and started massaging his balls.

"Hell yeah," he groaned.

When Ashanti deep throated Ahmad again, the way his legs began to shake informed her that he was about to reach his climax. Sure enough, within moments, he tried to move from her mouth, but she held him in place as she swallowed every drop of his cum. Ashanti's mouth never left his dick after she swallowed. She continued sucking until he was hard again. Once she was good and satisfied, Ashanti stood up, removed her clothes, and eased down on his awaiting dick. The feeling was indescribable. To Ashanti, it seemed as if each time Ahmad entered her it was better and better.

Just as she was about to cum, Ahmad flipped her over and took control.

"I want that shit in my mouth," he exclaimed right before he began sucking and biting her clit. As soon as he entered two fingers into her soaked pussy, she began to squirt, and Ahmad devoured her and swallowed as much as he possibly could. When her climax was ending, she felt Ahmad slide back inside her wetness. He stroked her until she came again and again. After he came inside of her, he laid down beside her and pulled her close.

"That's the only pussy I've had and even want since that kiss in New York," he said and kissed her on the forehead.

"I love you girl!" he told her.

"I love you too, baby," she replied and mentally told herself that she would continue to trust her man no matter what and to tell those hoes to kiss her ass.

After laying there and holding each other for about ten minutes, Ashanti got up so that she could go and use the bathroom. She went upstairs, washed up, and then grabbed one of Ahmad's tee shirts and put it on. Ashanti realized that she had left her phone in the truck, so she called down the stairs and asked Ahmad would he go and get it. A few minutes later, he walked up the stairs, entered his bedroom, and handed it to her. Ashanti noticed that Liyah had been blowing her up. She was about to call her, but decided to check the text messages first. The first message she saw pissed her off so bad that she slapped the shit out of Ahmad.

Chapter Seventeen

"Shanti... what the hell?" Ahmad asked as he rubbed his left cheek. Ashanti had just slapped the hell out of him and his shit was stinging something serious.

"Ahmad... I just told myself that I was gonna continue trusting you, but shit like this makes it fucking hard to do," Shanti screamed and threw her phone at Ahmad. By instinct, he caught it and wanted to slap his damn self when he looked at the picture that was displayed on the screen.

"What... what the..." Ahmad stuttered.

"Yeah... what the fuck was she doing in your bed Ahmad?" Shanti screamed.

"I know this shit looks bad... baby I know it does, but the fact still remains that I didn't fuck her," Ahmad affirmed.

"But why the fuck was she even in your bed Ahmad? This is some bullshit," Shanti fumed.

"She did come up one night. We were drinking and shit, and she got drunk..." he tried to explain before Ashanti cut him off.

"You know what, save this story because I don't wanna hear that shit right now. If y'all were drinking and shit, then there's a chance that you fucked her. I know how you are when you drink... which means the kid just might be yours Ahmad... I can't deal with this right now. I'll talk to you tomorrow," Ashanti said and walked out. Ahmad tried to grab her but her defeated look let him know that she really was adamant about getting away. He had no choice but to let her go, but he vowed that Sabrina wasn't going to come between them. Ahmad fell back onto his bed frustrated as fuck.

Ahmad laid there for about ten minutes before he got up. He knew that Ashanti would be pissed if he did or didn't chase after her. He was basically in a lose-lose situation, but she would just have to get over it. Laying there mad and moping around wasn't going to solve a damn thing, so he got his ass up and decided to head to her place. Ahmad grabbed his cell phone and placed a call to his homeboy as he headed out the door.

"What's up bruh?" Seth answered on the second ring.

"Man... the craziest shit just happened," Ahmad began.

"I can tell its some shit. I don't' know what it is, but I'm with Liyah, and we headed to Shanti's crib," Seth told him.

"Got dammit... I'm on my way too," Ahmad said and ended the call.

When Ahmad made it to Ashanti's place on South Montgomery, he turned in and saw Seth standing outside by Aaliyah's car. He parked and hopped out.

"Why you out here?" Ahmad asked as soon as he made it to his boy.

"Shit, Liyah told me to wait because Shanti probably wanted to talk alone. Plus, I knew you was on the way anyway, so I didn't even argue wit' her. What the hell happened though?" Seth asked.

"Maannn... Sabrina ass popped up at my crib big and pregnant," Ahmad stated, still seething about the incident.

"What the fuck? She pregnant? How far along is she? But what the hell that got to do wit' you?" Seth fired question after question after question.

"This twenty-one questions nigga?" Ahmad inquired and chuckled.

"But on the real, I'm tryna figure that shit out too," he continued.

Ahmad and Seth both stood there in silence for a few minutes trying to figure the shit out. They both were targets for gold diggers since they were NBA prospects. But, Ahmad couldn't figure out what Sabrina's angle could be since he never slept with her. He chunked it up to just trying to start some drama since they did kick it for a short period of time.

"Is it your baby?" Ahmad broke the silence by asking. He knew Seth had slept with her, which was one the many reasons he never fucked Sabrina.

"I strapped up man... and I ain't heard from that hoe in forever. She got what she wanted and dipped," Seth replied while shaking his head.

"I believe her ass just pissed off because I dropped her so fast. You better tell Liyah before she gets to her first man," Ahmad told his friend.

"Damn... me and Liyah wasn't even together at the time though. Sabrina better not come to me on no bullshit," Seth responded.

They continued talking about the shit, and before they knew it, an hour had passed. Ahmad looked up when he heard the door open and saw Aaliyah walk out. Ashanti was at the door watching her friend leave. She closed the door when Ahmad locked eyes with her.

"Did you fuck that hoe Ahmad?" Liyah asked as she approached them.

"I told her I didn't. I know the shit looks all bad because I did kick it wit' her, but I didn't fuck her," Ahmad replied with earnest.

"Okay... I'm just saying, if you did and it was before you and Shanti made everything official, then she will understand if you say it now. But if she find out you lying later on... she gonna put you in the same category as your dog ass brother. Just tell her if you did is all I'm saying," Liyah pleaded with him.

'I'm not gon' hurt Shanti... Ima always keep it one hundred wit' her. I know you got her back, but so do I," Ahmad replied.

"I know you do... I just had to say something though. You better get yo ass in there and make it right," Liyah told him and gave him a hug.

"I'll holla at y'all later," Ahmad said his goodbyes to Seth and Liyah and made his way inside. He was shocked that Shanti didn't lock the door. He walked in and found her sitting on the couch like she was waiting on him.
***

Seth offered to drive when Ahmad left them outside, and Aaliyah hurriedly agreed and made her way around to the passenger side. He tried to figure out which angle he needed to take. Seth knew enough about women to know that the advice they always gave their friends, they didn't always want or use it for themselves. Aaliyah was a good girl, but he knew that she was no different and was going to be pissed the fuck off if Sabrina's baby was his. He didn't think it was, but he contemplated Ahmad's words as he tried his best to figure out if he should throw it out there to keep her from being blindsided if anything popped off.

"I don't think Ahmad fucked that girl... he wouldn't lie about it. Sabrina gon get her ass whooped after she has that baby though," Aaliyah interjected. Seth looked over at her and saw that she was scrolling through Facebook.

"See… this shit here, she's such a scandalous hoe. Bitch done made a status talking 'bout her baby gon be a millionaire," Liyah fumed as she scrolled on her phone.

Seth continued driving while Liyah vented on and on about the situation. Her next comment caught him totally off guard.

"So is it your baby Seth?" she asked without prejudice.

"Huh?" was the only thing that would come out of his mouth.

"Oh, I think you heard me loud and clear. Them type of hoes always have motives. She look like the type that's just causing drama for Ahmad because he rejected her ass, but you probably the one that fucked her," Liyah stated as she stared at Seth.

By putting her phone down, he knew that she was serious and that the conversation was about to continue whether he wanted it to or not. Seth and Liyah didn't have many arguments at all, but he knew her well enough to know that when something was on her mind, she was going to get it off her chest right then and there. Seth sighed before he finally replied.

"Ok, I admit it. I did fuck her a couple times, but I strapped up each time. And just to be clear, that shit happened *waaay* before me and you even got together," he stressed.

"So if I didn't ask, were you gon' tell me?" Aaliyah calmly inquired.

"I was thinking 'bout it. I didn't know the girl was even pregnant until Ahmad just filled me in on everything," Seth truthfully replied.

"So you were thinking about whether to tell me or not… hoping that your name didn't pop up," Liyah retorted with a grim chuckle.

"It ain't like that babe… I'm just finding out, and people don't go around claiming babies and shit unless they know for sure," he replied as he tried to appeal to her.

"Okay," Liyah said and picked her phone back up and put her headphones in.

Seth could tell that she was pissed off by the way her legs were trembling. Their past arguments were over little simple shit, nothing to worry about. But this current state of affairs would more than likely be the biggest test that they faced as a couple, although they had not declared their relationship official or anything. This potential disastrous situation would either make them or break them.

Seth guaranteed that he was going to do everything he could to make it work because Aaliyah was it for him. She was everything that he was not looking for and more. She reached him and understood him on a level that no one ever had before. Even though he hadn't yet voiced it out loud to her, Seth really did love Aaliyah. Before, he was the one who fucked all of the groupies and wasn't thinking about settling down. But once Seth got a taste of Liyah and her sweet honey, it was no problem for him to cut off all of his past hoes because he could drink from *that* honey fountain for the rest of his life. He just prayed that would mean something to her once he explained how everything went down. He mentally prepared himself to go home and do some begging like Keith Sweat.

Chapter Eighteen

"How in the hell you gon' pull this off? You know damn well that fake ass pregnant belly ain't gon produce no baby," Meek said to her girl.

"How you know it ain't?" Sabrina replied as her girl gave her the *bitch please* look.

"Don't look at me like that… but I just wanna cause a lil drama. If I can get that bitch to leave him, Ahmad will fall right back into my arms," Sabrina continued.

"You think that man gon' want you, and you lying 'bout being pregnant? Then how you gon explain the nonexistent baby bitch?" Meek sarcastically inquired.

"I don't know, but yo ass supposed to be helping me think instead of criticizing me," Sabrina snidely remarked.

"You know I'm always down for some drama, but you thought of the dumbest shit on earth. I just don't see your logic with this, but we shall see," Meek replied and threw her hands up in defeat.

Sabrina ignored the rest of her home girl's stares and comments and continued driving towards her apartment in Starkville Plaza. When she turned into the complex, kids were still outside playing like it was not after eleven o'clock at night. Sabrina drove all the way down to the opposite end since her apartment was in the last building and parked.

"You ain't leaving the fake belly in the car this time?" Meek asked her and laughed.

"Nope…I need people to start seeing me carrying the child of Ahmad Jones for these next two months," Sabrina replied and got out of the car and wobbled inside.

"Brina hoe ass done got pregnant!" someone said in the distance.

"I guess so, but I don't know who fucked her without a condom," another voice stated.

"Fuck y'all!" Sabrina replied and stormed into her apartment.

Meek walked in behind her laughing her ass off.

"I'm bout sick of yo ass for the day anyways," Sabrina told her as she took off her fake pregnant belly and threw it on the couch.

She ordered it online about a month back. She got the idea one day while watching a show where men wore fake pregnant bellies to emulate and empathize with their pregnant women as they try to walk in their women's shoes. Sabrina lit up a blunt and began smoking right away as she tried to figure out exactly how she was going to execute her next move.

"Don't worry… I'm 'bout to get away from yo delusional ass," Meek replied, laughing her tail off at her crazy ass friend.

Sabrina pulled her phone from her pocket and scrolled to the pictures she had taken of Ahmad while he was sleep. She had enough pictures both real and photo shopped to fuck with Ashanti for days, and she planned on doing just that. When Ahmad went to the bathroom one day, Sabrina picked up his phone. Since he had just put it down, it had not locked yet, and she was able to retrieve Ashanti's phone number. She wanted to puke when she noticed that he had it saved as 'My Queen' but that only made her want him that much more.

"He's gonna be mine very soon," Sabrina mumbled to herself. She was so lost in her thoughts that she didn't even see her friend leave or hear her say goodbye. After she laughed to herself, she sent one picture and sat back and waited for the fireworks to explode.

Chapter Nineteen

The back and forth trips to Greenville had been working out very smooth for Kentay for the past few months. He kept his word and saw Kendall at least once a week, sometimes more when he made extra time. Since he had missed six years of his life, he did everything he could to make up for lost time. Eventually, he wanted both of his kids to meet, but he was waiting on the correct timing.

"You want some ice cream?" Kentay asked his son after he ran over and got a sip of his Hi-C orange drink. It was Friday evening, and they were at McDonald's. Kendall was playing and having a blast. Kentay picked him up right after school to spend a few hours with him because Courtney told him they had plans for the weekend.

"The machine is always broken," Kendall replied and took off again to go and play. Kentay couldn't do anything but laugh at him because McDonald's was known for their ice cream machines to always be down. Kentay's phone chimed with a text message, and he figured it was Courtney. He looked down and confirmed it.

Courtney: Y'all okay?

Kentay: All the time baby girl

Courtney: Just checking... you know how I am. I'll be home in about an hour.

Kentay: Aight. You need anything?

Courtney: Yep... I'll let you know what later ☺

Kentay: Don't start no shit lol

Kentay couldn't believe the changes that he had made in his life. Thoughts of killing Courtney never even entered his mind anymore. Had it been a year ago when he saw her, he was pretty sure that he would be in jail for murder. Time sure does bring about changes. As soon as Kentay placed his phone down, it rang. It was Slick calling to fill him in on some important information. Kentay listened closely all the while doing a mental countdown of what was to come. They talked for about five minutes, and when Kentay hung up, he called Kendall to come on so that he could get him home. He planned on taking him to see a movie but rain checked the plans since Courtney had to get on the road to Memphis; she was going to visit her mom.

Courtney was sitting on the couch when Kentay walked in. She must have heard him pull up in the driveway because the door was already unlocked. Kentay noticed that she looked extremely tired, and it appeared that she had been crying.

"What's wrong?" he genuinely asked her.

"Do you feel bad again, mommy?" Kendall asked his mom and then went and hugged her.

'I'm fine, baby," she replied, but Kentay could tell that she was putting on a front. As he stood there and watched the interaction between Courtney and Kendall, he reflected on some of Courtney's actions that he had previously shrugged off. He had noticed how tired she was and how weak she appeared on some days, how her appetite was sometimes nonexistent, and how much weight she had lost in just the past month alone. He asked her about it one time, and she told him that the job had become stressful so he shrugged it off. But now, as he saw how clingy Kendall was to her and the things he said to her, Kentay surmised that something deeper was wrong. As soon as Kendall went to his room, Kentay began firing questions at Courtney in attempt to get to the bottom of things, but she continued to dodge his questions and insisted that nothing was wrong and declared that she was fine. He had no choice but to let it go for the moment, but he definitely planned on finding out what the real deal was. The whole way home that night, his mind was on ways to figure out exactly what the problem was. Kentay was thankful that he had made some connections while in prison and planned on hitting one of them up as soon as possible.

The next day, Kentay personally went and checked on his spots. It was now time to show his face and get shit popping. He had already put his biggest plan in motion, and as soon as night fell, it was going to be on.

"What the hell? Yooo nigga what… how… dammmnnn is it really you?" Dub stated excitedly as soon as Kentay walked into the spot in Rock Hill.

"The one and only!" Kentay grinned and gave him a brotherly hug.

"I'm so glad to see you… shit been crazy as fuck. You just getting out?" Dub asked him.

"Not really... I had to check out some shit and stay low when I first blew that joint, but I'm back now, and it's time to rectify some shit," Tay responded.

"Say no more," Dub replied and nodded his head.

When night fell, Kentay headed out to a spot down in Crawford, where he had set some shit up. What he was about to do had to be done, and he let Slick know that he needed to be the one to handle it for several reasons. Buck was his blood and had played him. In addition, he also shot his brother, so Kentay wanted to do the honors of sending him to meet his maker. Buck thought that he was about to meet with a new connect, but he was about to get the surprise of his life in a few short minutes. Kentay speculated that he would be strapped but that wasn't a concern to him. He knew how the game went and told himself it is what it is, even though he had no plans on leaving anyway other than the way he came.

Slick and Dub were actually already in the spot awaiting Kentay's arrival. When Buck so eagerly agreed to a meeting location, time, day, and everything without any questions, Kentay knew that he was an amateur and would never be boss status. When he pulled up to the location, his throw away phone rang. He knew who was on the other end without even answering. Kentay sent the call to voicemail and sent Buck a text telling him he was about to walk in. Five minutes later, dressed in all black, Kentay turned the knob and walked inside. As soon as he walked in, a gun was placed to his head, but Kentay showed no fear.

"This how you treat ya fam man?" Kentay casually inquired.

"Tay? Is that you?" Buck asked and then flipped the light switch on.

"Who you thought it was meeting you at this spot?" Tay asked and pushed Buck's gun away from him and went and sat down on the couch.

"Bruh... them niggas Slick and Dub been gunning for me, and I don't know why. I really thought it was them pussies tryna play me. Mu'fucka's even blew my house up," Buck rambled on and on.

"Slick and Dub? Them niggas wanna be me so bad... that's probably why they gunning for you so hard because they know you next in command after me," Kentay replied in an attempt to get Buck to let his guards down.

"That's what I'm saying cuz!" Buck retorted.

"So what you do when they blew yo shit up? I know you ain't let that shit ride," Kentay continued to egg him on.

"Hell naw... this shit ain't over. I thought I got Slick ass, but it wasn't him. I did a drive by but came up short," Buck stated with frustration in his voice.

"I heard about that. That was you, fam?" Tay asked to confirm what he already knew.

"Yeah... killed some random nigga and shot up another. That basketball player... Jones or whatever the fuck his name is. But, oh fuckin' well! He was in the wrong place at the wrong time... you know how shit go sometimes," Buck replied and shrugged his shoulders. Kentay watched him as he picked up a drink and gulped it down.

"So what would you do if that was your brother that was shot in a random drive by?" Kentay asked in a laid-back way.

"I would find the mu'fuckas that did it and light they asses up," Buck replied with authority.

"I know you would... anyway, let's get down to business," Tay said and patted the seat next to him. He watched as Buck sat the gun down on the table and made his way to sit on the couch. Kentay had to shake his head at his cousin's stupidity. When Buck sat down, Kentay fed him a little bullshit until he grew tired of playing games. He reached under the cushion of the couch and pulled his gun out. Before Buck knew what was going on, Kentay stood in front of him with a gun to his dome. Kentay whistled and watched as Dub and Slick strolled out of their hiding locations.

"It's three reasons why you going to meet yo maker tonight you pussy ass nigga," Tay calmly stated.

"Wai... wait... what's..." Buck stuttered.

"Shut the fuck up! Yo talk time is over," Kentay spat.

"One... you stole from me after I did nothing but help yo grimy ass," Kentay said, and Slick fired off a shot that hit Buck in his left leg, and he cried like a bitch. He tried to get up and run, but Kentay hit him in the head with the gun and forced him back down on the couch.

"Two... you just a pussy ass nigga!" Kentay said, and Dub fired a shot that hit Buck in the right leg. He cried even more.

"Three… just like you said if yo brother was shot, you would find them mu'fuckas and light 'em up… well Ahmad Jones is my brother mu'fucka!" Kentay barked and fired two shots to Buck's dome, silencing him forever.

Chapter Twenty

Time had passed by, but it didn't heal the wounds like people had told him it would. In fact, it seemed like things had only gotten worse because the people who should have paid dearly for Raven's death seemed to be living it up in Jason's eyes. He couldn't allow himself to sit back any longer without taking matters into his own hands. Jason watched Cynthia day in and out for the past month, studying her every move. She always kept a smile on her face. When she left home, she would frequent different hotels, and he assumed that she was entertaining men. It was obvious that she didn't work, but she stayed in designer clothes, drove a Mercedes, and had what appeared to be a three or four bedroom house built out in the country.

One day while she was out, Jason broke into Cynthia's home in search of some answers on how she maintained such a lavish lifestyle with no job. When he walked in, he heard a beeping noise and figured out that it was coming from an alarm. He immediately pulled out his pocket knife, opened the alarm, and cut the wires. The beeping stopped instantly, and Jason proceeded forward. Jason admired the home and his anger began rising. Cynthia had always treated Raven like shit. After Raven died, she really started living life. Jason made his way to what had to be the master bedroom. He looked under the bed and saw a safety deposit box and grabbed it.

After Jason opened the box and read everything inside, it didn't take him long to figure out how Cynthia was living so well. The first thing he saw was a wad of money; however, the important paper located beneath the wad of money caught his eye. It was a life insurance policy for five hundred thousand dollars. Jason immediately attempted to figure out how Cynthia cashed in a life insurance policy when Raven committed suicide. The next paper was a copy of the autopsy, and it showed the cause of death was a heart attack. He picked up an envelope and inside it was a receipt for fifty thousand dollars. The name on the receipt looked familiar. When Jason looked back at the other paper, it was confirmed that it was to the same name listed on the autopsy report. It pissed him off that Cynthia had made a way to benefit herself through her daughter's death.

As he sat there on her bed, he became angrier by the second. Jason heard the front door slam. He was so pissed off that he never heard Cynthia pull up. Jason jumped up and got in the closet as quickly as he could when he heard footsteps heading towards the bedroom. He didn't even bother to push the safety deposit box back under the bed. Jason watched as Cynthia looked down at the box.

"What the hell?" she quizzically inquired.

"Yeah... what the hell is the million dollar question?" Jason said as he exited the closet. Cynthia jumped and when she reached towards the nightstand, Jason rushed over to her and pushed her face down onto the bed.

"Don't move and don't scream!" he stated through gritted teeth.

"Now, we can do this the easy way or the hard way," he continued as he pulled Cynthia up by the hair. He turned her around and then pushed her back on the bed and started asking her questions.

"Did you ever love your daughter? How could you look for ways to get money through her death? You been waiting on her to die, haven't you?" he asked her. When she didn't answer fast enough, he slapped the taste out of her mouth, literally.

"I asked you some questions, so I suggest you answer," Jason calmly said.

"The little bitch didn't care about me, so why should I care about her. Why shouldn't I benefit from the life insurance policy that I had been paying for all these years? I always knew she was suicidal because of her disorder, so I had a plan," Cynthia snidely replied.

"You kidnapping her baby didn't help so you can't blame me for everything," she taunted.

When she said that, it was like a light went off in Jason's head. His emotions began to race all over the place. He already had partially blamed himself for her death, which was why he sought therapy. He loved Raven and to hear those words come from someone who admittedly didn't give a damn about her, set him off. Before he knew it, his hands were wrapped around Cynthia's neck. She gasped for air and struggled to fight him off. However, he was in a blackout zone and her cries fell upon deaf ears. Jason literally squeezed her throat until she turned black and blue. Cynthia stopped moving and breathing. He fell back onto to the floor and stared at her lifeless body for hours. As he stared, Jason began to formulate his next stage of revenge.

Chapter Twenty-One

Ashanti wasn't going to believe that her father was alive for sure until she saw him face to face. She had been going through the motions about everything, but decided that it was finally time to get off of her ass and put some shit in order. The bullshit with Sabrina had her pissed off at Ahmad for a few days, but she couldn't stay mad at him much longer. They talked and agreed that they would handle whatever else they may be presented with together. Ahmad had an out of town game, which included Seth, so he couldn't travel with her to see her dad. Their season opener was the week before, and they started the season off with a win. So instead of Ahmad, Aaliyah rode with Ashanti to the Mississippi State Penitentiary.

♫**Jump in the Cadillac... girl let's put some miles on it**
Anything you want... just to put a smile on you
You deserve it baby, you deserve it all
And I'm gonna give it to you...
Gold jewelry be shining so bright
Strawberry champagne on ice
Lucky for you, that's what I like, that's what I like
Lucky for you, that's what I like, what I like
Sex by the fire at night
Silk sheets and diamonds all white
Lucky for you, that's what I like, what I like
Lucky for you, that's what I like, what I like.♫

Shanti and Liyah sang along with Bruno Mars to the top of their lungs.

"This is my new favorite song!" Shanti exclaimed when it went off.

"I love it too girl." Liyah eagerly agreed.

When the song ended, Liyah went back to being quiet, causing Ashanti to turn off the radio so they could talk.

"Okay... tell me what's wrong? You been acting odd for about a week now. I'm supposed to be the one walking around looking like a sad puppy dog with this baby shit, but you talked me into trusting Ahmad. And not to mention, my stomach in knots because I don't know what I'm 'bout to walk into in the next hour," Shanti stated.

"I hate to even bring it up because I know your mind is on a lot too," Liyah replied very solemn.

"Girl, if you don't cut the shit and tell me what's wrong," Shanti reiterated.

"I been tryna make myself take my own advice, but the shit is hard as hell. But how about that damn baby might be Seth's!" Liyah finally admitted after sighing, exasperated.

"What the hell? How did you find that out?" Shanti quizzically inquired.

"Just call it women's intuition. I could tell it was something by how he was acting that night we left your place, and then I just came right out and asked him. Seth being Seth, he admitted that he slept with her a couple times but strapped up each time. Hell, you know that shit don't mean nothing—condoms break. But anyways, I think that hoe is just tryna cause problems for you because she wants Ahmad. I don't think he slept with her, his buddy sure did though," Liyah replied, filled with a lot of frustration and irritation.

"Damn... well it's like you told me... you gotta stick wit' him until you know. As big as she is, it had to be before your time. It's still fucked up, but you can't let the thots win," Shanti stated.

"I'm trying to do that... I finally talked to him today so I'm making progress," Liyah told her friend. They continued talking without music for the remainder of the ride, giving each other pep talks. Ashanti followed Siri's instructions and navigated onto the premises before she knew it. She had to use her google maps since Ahmad drove her the first time, and she wasn't paying any attention.

Ashanti got out and made her way inside while Aaliyah stayed in the truck. After walking inside and getting through the line, Ashanti made her way to the visitation room, and the first person she locked eyes with was her mom. She saw her getting up from a table in the corner near the back. Now, she knew why her mom told her the best time to visit was around one o'clock. Ashanti was an hour early and figured that her mom must have wanted to visit first without her knowing. She noticed a glow on her mom's face that she hadn't seen in years, if ever. Ashanti slowly made her way to the back. She figured her mom was still standing there since she had been caught.

The closer that Ashanti got to the table, the faster her heart beat. Tears started flowing down her face when her eyes met her dad's. She never knew that her feet had stopped moving until she felt his arms around her. Big Al pulled Ashanti into a bear hug that lasted for minutes. When he finally let go, Ashanti noticed that he had been crying too, along with Tina. Once she finally sat down next to her dad, she was speechless. Tina broke the silence a few minutes later by telling them that she was about to leave and let them have some alone time. Ashanti and Big Al were too caught up in each other to respond but Big Al acknowledged her with a nod.

"I really… I really just can't believe I'm actually looking at you," Ashanti sobbed and finally broke their silence.

"It seems unreal. I have dreamt about this day so many times," Big Al emotionally expressed and got choked up. Ashanti looked at him and could tell that he was an emotional wreck, but doing his best to hold it in. After a few minutes, they both got themselves together and were able to talk and catch up. Ashanti felt like there would never be enough time in the world for them to make up for all of the years they lost. She listened as her dad explained the situation about Kya to her as well as her grandparents and why he didn't want to her to have any resentment towards her mom for the choice that she made. He even told her about a few of things that he had been through while on the inside. Some of it included his dealings with Kentay and also the incident Kya had been involved in. She could tell that he was holding back and not telling her every single detail by how he guarded his words but guessed there had to be a reason behind it.

Ashanti couldn't help but to feel like there was an underlying message in what he was saying, but she couldn't figure it out. A loud buzzer went off, and a guard notified everyone that visitation time was over. She got up and hugged her dad and didn't let go until he painfully broke away from her.

"Take care of your mom. Be there for your sister. Ahmad is a keeper. I love you, and I'll be in touch," Big Al said to Ashanti before she walked away. Ashanti smiled and told him that she loved him too as a fresh batch of tears began to flow.

Chapter Twenty-Two

"It is so beautiful here. This is gon' be the best fall break ever!" Amanda exclaimed as she took pictures of the clear blue water from the balcony of their resort in Puerto Rico.

"I want every moment we spend together to be the best," Slick disclosed as he came up behind Amanda and hugged her from the back. She squirmed when he placed soft kisses on the back of her neck.

"You're just too sweet. I love you," Amanda purred.

"And I love you back," Slick honestly replied, acknowledging it for the first time to her.

Amanda turned around and wrapped her arms around her man and looked into his sexy eyes. She was so glad that he had surprised her with a vacation because school was kicking her ass the current semester. Amanda had been stretched to the max with school and going back and forth to Starkville every chance she got not only to see Slick, but mostly Kya. The only thing Amanda had on was a yellow bikini and Slick had on a pair of shorts. Their plan was to walk down to the pool area and get in for a little while, but Amanda changed her mind once she felt the bulge between Slick's legs as she kissed him.

After tugging at Slick's shorts, they both looked at each other and knew what the deal was. Amanda gently pushed him down onto the chaise that was on the balcony. The eagerness by Amanda was evident as she hurriedly kneeled down and took Slick's long, hard, and thick shaft into her mouth. She had watched some porn a few days before, and she was ready to test out a new trick that she saw. Amanda thought back to how the girl had a whole dick in her mouth sucking while using her tongue to lick the man's balls. Her first two attempts were an epic fail, but the third time was a charm. She knew that she was doing it right by the reaction she got from Slick. Inwardly smiling, she continued to please her man until she was ready to feel him inside of her.

Amanda stood up and tried to ease down on Slick's dick, but he had other plans. He stood up, made her lean over the balcony, and then entered her from the back. Amanda couldn't control the screams that escaped her mouth as he hit her spot with every single stroke. Amanda looked down and saw a couple looking up at her, and surprisingly, it turned her on. Her and Slick put on a show for the next twenty minutes until they both came and fell back onto the chaise and laughed at the memory they had just made.

The next morning, the smell of bacon woke Amanda up from her sleep. She smiled because Slick always did everything in his power to make her happy. He remembered the little things and knew that bacon was her favorite breakfast food. As soon as he sat down beside her on the bed, Amanda's stomach began to bubble, and she felt nauseous. No longer able to hold the contents that were making their way back up her esophagus, Amanda hopped up off of the bed and made a dash for the bathroom. After she emptied all of the contents from her stomach into the toilet, she got up, washed her face, and brushed her teeth. Slick stood at the door watching her every move.

"You okay babe? The bacon wasn't that burnt… you done hurt my feelings," Slick playfully stated after Amanda finished and walked towards him.

"I'm fine. Must be that food from last night. No worries though baby… I'm 'bout to tear this bacon up," she replied and forced a smile at him.

As soon as Amanda sat back down on the bed, the smell of the food hit her again, but she forced herself not to throw up again. It was hard as hell, but some kind of way she made it through. Slick eyed her very carefully and kept asking her if she was alright, and she continued to tell him 'yes.' Amanda didn't know what was wrong with her. She knew that she wasn't pregnant because she took her birth control pills like clockwork every night. After switching to a new kind the last month, she started taking them at night instead of in the morning, but she figured that shouldn't have affected anything.

Amanda and Slick made it through breakfast and proceeded to get dressed for the day. He had a list of different activities that they could engage in but left the decision up to her. They both dressed comfortably because neither of them knew what the day would bring. After looking through the brochures, Amanda decided that they should parasailing first. Slick was totally against the idea at first, but after a few kisses and puppy dog eyes, Amanda finally got him to give in.

"That shit was actually fun, but I ain't doing it no mo," Slick announced after they purchased the CD with pictures that were taken while they were eight hundred feet in the air.

"I would definitely do it again. Don't be a punk," Amanda teased him.

"Don't even play. You know good and damn well I ain't no punk," Slick goaded.

"Yeah, I know all too well," Amanda replied and then pulled him in for a kiss.

"Don't start no shit out here," Slick retorted as he broke the kiss.

Amanda smirked at him and then pranced away. Amanda was tired and ready to go relax, but Slick talked her into doing some shopping. He told her that he wanted to splurge on her. After trying on tons of clothing and admiring herself in them, Slick purchased them all. When he picked up a couple of baby outfits, Amanda was stunned and had no idea what he was doing.

"Who are those for?" she asked him, puzzled.

"For our baby that you're carrying," he simply replied.

"Boy... I ain't pregnant," Amanda asserted and shrugged him off.

"You pregnant and don't even know it," Slick happily replied.

"I'm on the pill baby... and I know you don't want any kids right now. I take my pills faithfully because I ain't tryna trap you or nothing," Amanda responded in all sincerity.

"We'll stop and get a test before we head back to the resort... but I can't be trapped anyway. You just get ready to be extra careful while you carrying my seed," Slick adamantly stated and headed out of the door.

Amanda looked at him like he was crazy but followed closely behind him. She decided to get the test just to shut him up, knowing that it was going to turn up negative. They only had unprotected sex a few times, plus she popped her pills daily. They had never even talked about kids, but Amanda could tell that Slick was already excited. The love and affection that he showed her, she knew that he would be great with kids but told herself that it wouldn't be any time soon. She just hoped that he wouldn't be too disappointed when the test proved him wrong.

An hour later, Amanda was shocked as hell as she stared at the pink plus sign on the pregnancy test. To say that she was shocked was really an understatement. Slick picked her up and twirled her around.

"Y'all won't have to worry about shit! I got my queen and my lil princess for life," he proudly guffawed.

"I can't believe I'm pregnant. OMG!" Amanda yelled, feeling terrified and skeptical of the results simultaneously.

"Wait… how you know it's a girl?" she continued, still in disbelief.

"I just know," he soothed and pulled her close to him.

They talked fervently and Amanda was finally excited as Slick was once she saw how elated he was. She was still nervous, but she knew that he would take care of her no matter what. Slick laid her down and made love to her until the sun came up. Later on that night, as they laid in bed and mapped out what they were going to do on their last day, Slick received a phone call that required his attention. Amanda didn't know what had gone wrong with that call. The only thing she knew was they were on a jet headed back home within the next hour because something bad had happened, but she was too afraid to ask what.

Chapter Twenty-Three

After Kentay found out exactly what was going on with Courtney, initially, he was extremely belligerent because he felt like she should have been honest with him. The more he thought about it, he began to understand her logic behind her decision to stay mute; he still didn't agree with it, but he understood it. It took money for him to get the ball rolling, but Kentay made preparations for Courtney to see a patient navigator in Jackson with the American Cancer Society that was stationed at the University of Mississippi Medical Center's Cancer Institute , and the information he researched had named the dwelling as the best facility in the area.

Kentay made reservations for Courtney to stay at the Marriott on the days that she had treatments to keep from traveling back and forth. On Friday, Kentay made a trip to Greenville and checked Kendall out of school at noon. He finally made up his mind to introduce his two children to each other. His dad was going to have Kendra already so everything was working out perfect. Courtney was scheduled for a treatment that morning, and he was taking Kendall to visit her that night before he headed back to Starkville, unless he decided to stay.

"How was school lil homie?" Kentay asked Kendall after he was settled into his truck and they were on their way.

"It was good. I learned all of my multiplication tables and got some extra stars," Kendall replied, excited about his accomplishments.

"Good job... I gotta reward you too. What you want?" Kentay inquired.

"Just for my mommy to not be sick anymore," Kendall replied in a sad voice and with tears in his little eyes as he bowed his head down.

Kentay was stunned by his reply, and he knew that he would continue to do everything to make his son's request happen; but, he couldn't make any promises.

"I'm gonna do everything I can to make that happen okay," Kentay stated and Kendall smiled and told him okay.

"Remember I told you that you had a baby sister? Are you ready to meet her?" Kentay asked his son. He saw Kendall's eyes light up as he nodded his head 'yes.' Kentay stopped by Wendy's and grabbed Kendall something to eat and then proceeded on to Jackson.

After Kendall finished eating his burger and fries, he fell asleep about ten minutes later. It was just Kentay and his music as he coasted down the highway. Kentay looked over at his sleeping son and realized just how much his life had changed within the past few months. He had been out of prison for a couple of months and felt like a new man. Although he was still handling business in the streets, Slick called most of the shots, the reason why Kentay had broken him off with some extra cash and forced him to get away for the weekend. With Dub on the team, the three of them were a force to be reckoned with, and each of them could handle shit with or without the other.

Two hours later, Tay was turning into his dad's driveway. When he saw a Range Rover like the one he had bought for Ashanti, except it was a different color, he put two and two together and realized that she had gotten rid of the one he had bought her and had gotten one on her own. Ashanti's bank account was sitting pretty thanks to him, but he knew that she deserved all of it after the hell he had taken her through. When Kentay parked, he briefly wondered how the introduction was about to go. He assumed that it would only be him, Dennis, and the kids present. After sitting there contemplating for a few minutes, he finally said *fuck it*, woke Kendall up, and headed inside.

Kentay walked to the door and like always, Dennis opened it before he could knock. Dennis looked down at Kendall and then back up at Kentay.

"Well you sure do know how to mark your kids," Dennis chuckled before he started talking to Kendall. Kentay stepped around him and his eyes locked with Ashanti's.

"I didn't know about him until…" Tay started to say before she cut him off.

"You don't have to explain anything to me. I guess it took having kids to mature you. That's good," Ashanti told him and then directed her attention back to Kendra, who was sitting in her lap.

Before Kentay could reply, Ahmad walked into the living room from towards the back of the house, and Kentay spoke to him instead of responding to Ashanti's comment. He felt like it was a low blow but bit his tongue because he deserved it. When Ashanti lost their baby, he was on vacation. Kentay didn't know how or what he could do to show Ashanti how sorry he was, but he was willing to do anything.

"That's your lil man there? He looks just like you," Ahmad told Kentay as he stared at his nephew.

"Yeah... that's the lil homie. I wanted him to meet his sister. I'm tryna do the right thing these days," Kentay countered, being modest about the situation.

"That's what's up. You mind if I holla at you for a minute?" Ahmad requested.

Kentay told him no problem and then they headed towards the back of the house. Ahmad led him downstairs to Dennis' man cave. It was equipped with a sixty inch flat screen mounted on the wall, a pool table, a black leather sectional, endless liquor, and other amenities. Kentay was inspired by his dad's man cave and planned on having one for himself in the future.

"Your lil man looks just like you. Kendra too," Ahmad added to break the ice.

"I can't even deny that... how you been though? Besides ballin' on the court. I'll be at the next home game," Kentay answered back.

"Just tryna make it, but I did wanna talk to you 'bout something. I know I ain't got to, but just outta respect because of this crazy relationship... I feel like its best," Ahmad remarked in a serious tone.

"What's up?" Kentay nervously questioned,

"I know that you love Shanti, but I feel like she was made for me. I can't imagine my life without her. I live, eat, breathe for her. I love her with everything in me. She really completes me, and I'm gonna ask her to marry me," Ahmad honestly stated.

Kentay froze and stood silent for a few moments. He had a feeling that this day would come, but he just didn't know it would be this soon. Deep down, he knew that Ahmad was the better man for Ashanti. He had already backed off and stopped all of his madness of pursuing her in any type of way. Kentay briefly thought about what he could finally do to repay Ashanti for all the grief that he had caused her, and he knew what he had to do.

"Wow...damn! I knew this was coming, but I ain't go lie... you just knocked the shit outta me with that. But it's all good though... You definitely deserve her. I respect you that much more for even running it by me bro... I really do. I wish you two nothing but the best," Kentay finally recovered from the surprised conversation and then stepped forward to give Ahmad a genuine hug. After the hug, he felt a feeling that he couldn't describe. He couldn't put his finger on it, but he felt good.

"I haven't decided exactly when I'm gonna ask her, but I picked out the ring already," Ahmad said and pulled a box out of his pocket.

"Daammmmnnnnn... that shit is nice as hell," Kentay admired when Ahmad opened the box and showed him the rock.

"She deserves it... and it's almost like mom knew something was about to happen to her because she had so much stuff laid out. You remember she did her own obituary, but she also wrote me a letter. She confirmed that Ashanti is the one... and how about she is the one who told me where to go and get this ring," Ahmad stated, still in awe by his mother's actions.

Kentay admired his brother's strength through everything that he had gone though. He had also lost his mom, so he related to him and regretted the way that he acted at the funeral. Even though they had made up and were working on their brotherly relationship, Kentay still felt like an asshole.

"I'm happy for you. I really am," Kentay told him.

"I appreciate it. And this might be a stretch, but you wanna be in the wedding," Ahmad asked, astounding his self with his request.

"Oohhh... man... you gon have to let me think about that," Kentay replied and laughed while rubbing the back of his head.

"Shanti might not like that," he conceded.

"She doesn't speak badly about you. I'm asking as a brother, but if you don't feel comfortable, I do understand," Ahmad genuinely replied.

"Alright, man, lemme think on this some more before I give you an answer," Tay answered back, feeling disjointed about this whole scenario.

"I can do that. Bet! On the real, thanks bro for hearing me out," Ahmad countered and pulled his bro in for another hug.

They talked for a few more minutes before they finally went back upstairs. Kentay smiled when he saw the interaction between Kendra and Kendall. In that moment, he knew that everything had turned out just the way it was supposed to and not how he wanted it to or thought it should. He was filled with joy and made a mental note to tell his brother that he would be honored to be in his wedding the next time they saw each other. He didn't want to bring it up at the moment because Ahmad hadn't popped the question yet, and Ashanti was clueless. After Ahmad and Ashanti left, Kentay allowed the kids to bond for another hour and a half before he left and took Kendall to his mom. When he saw that Courtney was okay and left his son with her, he headed on back to Starkville.

Later that night, Kentay made a run to Rock Hill so that he could retrieve the money from the safe. Dub had hit him up and told him that all of the product in the areas was gone and that it would be close to midnight before he got back in town. Kentay told him that he would pick up the money since Slick was out of town on a much needed getaway. When Kentay pulled up, he looked at the clock and noticed that it was a quarter to midnight. With the intentions on only running in and out, Kentay left his truck on and proceeded inside.

Just as Kentay was about to open the safe, he heard the front door open and close. He reached in his pocket and realized that he had left his gun under the seat.

"Fuck... this better be Dub," he said as he walked back towards the front and called out to Dub. If it wasn't him, he knew that he needed to get to one of the several guns that were stashed throughout the house.

"Dub!" Kentay called out again.

"Nope. It's not Dub," the voice replied.

As soon as Kentay rounded the corner, his eyes met the barrel of a gun. He looked at the man holding the gun, and he looked familiar, but Kentay couldn't place him.

"You looking like you don't know who I am," the man calmly stated.

"Nigga, I don't know who the fuck you are and clearly you don't know who the fuck I am," Kentay seethed.

"I know exactly who you are. You're the reason Raven is dead, you pathetic piece of shit," Jason spat with much venom.

It was in that moment that Kentay realized exactly who was standing before him. He remembered Raven talking about him before and knew that he had some issues. Kentay saw his life flash before his eyes. He knew that all of the things he had done had finally come back to haunt him. A car light flashed outside, but Kentay didn't know who it was because a shot to the chest sent him backwards and then to the floor. Jason stood over him and pointed the gun at his head.

"That was for Raven and this is for me," Jason terrorized and fired another shot. Kentay thought he heard the sound of Dub's voice and thought Jason fell to the floor, but he wasn't sure because everything got black and went silent.
***

Since Dub had to make a run out to Tuscaloosa, he sent Kentay a text and told him to pick up the money later that night because he wasn't sure if he would make it back before midnight. The transition he went to take care of was smooth, so he grabbed something to eat from Burger King on the way out. The lady in the drive thru wore a bow tie and manager's outfit, and she was eye fucking him. When she wrote her number down on his receipt, Dub smiled and made a mental note to hit her up the next time that he was in town.

Dub turned his music back up and *Broccoli* by DRAM was playing, and he sang along with it. "I'm beyond all that fuck shit… hey" Dub sang like the lyrics were made just for him. He made the drive back to Starkville, and something told him to head to Rock Hill. So instead of going home, he followed his mind. When Dub got ready to turn into the trap house, he noticed an unfamiliar car parked in the yard as well as Kentay's truck. He pulled his gun from underneath his seat and checked his pocket to make sure the other one was secure because something didn't feel right to him.

After he saw the door was cracked, he really got an eerie feeling. A voice that he didn't recognize could be heard as he crept inside slowly. A gunshot sounded and Dub knew that he had to speed up his pace.

"That was for Raven and this is for me," that same voice said again. By that time, Dub had his gun pointed at the back of an unidentified man's head. He fired a shot, but he also saw his boy go down, so he figured he must have been a split second too late.

"Fuck!" Dub angrily yelled as he made his way over to Kentay. He didn't know who the other man was, but he knew that ole dude was dead, and he needed to get his homie to the hospital right away. Dub tried not to panic as he looked down at all of the blood that was pouring from Kentay's chest and the second shot looked like it was near his neck, but there was so much blood that Dub couldn't be sure. Dub couldn't call the police to that particular location, so he ran and pulled Kentay's truck near the door since it was the closest and still running. Dub grabbed all of the blankets that he could and picked Kentay up. It scared him when he didn't hear him moan or respond to him, so he hurried his pace. Dub mentally outlined what needed to happen and coached himself to take Kentay to the hospital first and then call the cleanup crew immediately afterwards.

Dub made it to the hospital in record time with the emergency lights on. He didn't know if the story he had in his head was going to work or even made sense, but he had to get his boy to the hospital right away and would deal with the police later. Dub parked right at the emergency entrance and jumped out. When the staff saw blood all over him, they jumped up right away. He led them to Kentay, and they put him on a gurney and rushed back inside. Dub told them that Kentay was his brother and that he was also Ahmad Jones' brother because he wanted them to do all they could. He heard the staff saying something about being airlifted to Tupelo or Jackson, and he knew that shit had just gotten real.

Chapter Twenty-Four

After Ashanti and Ahmad returned from Jackson, she went in her closet and started looking for something to wear for later that night. Her and Aaliyah planned on going to a place they heard about called *Sopranos*, located in West Point, to relax and have a little fun. The establishment was highlighted as a spot for mature young adults and adults, so they wouldn't have to worry about the crowds that normally frequent places like Level III and VIP (also known as The Hunt Club). Ahmad and Seth planned on chilling at Seth's place to play video games, but she was desperate and needed some girl time. It was long overdue. While searching for an outfit, Ashanti had an idea, so she picked up her phone and texted Kya, who texted right back in an instance.

Ashanti: Hey Kya... what you up to?

Kya: Hey Shanti... not a thing. Laying here watching TV.

Ashanti: Well get dressed. You're going out with me and Liyah.

Kya: Going out where? I might not have anything to wear.

Ashanti: You have all kinda cute clothes... don't play. I'm throwing on some ripped jeans and a top with a blazer. It's a chill spot and you need to get outta the house.

Kya: Don't seem like I have a choice so I'll find something. What time should I come over?

Ashanti: I can pick you up about 9:30

Kya: Okay.

After Ashanti finished texting Kya, she laid her clothes out on the bed and went to hop in the shower. As soon as she took her clothes off and stepped into the shower, she heard the door open and she jumped and screamed.

"Who else you think gon' be walking up in here?" Ahmad asked her.

"Shit... I thought you were gone," Shanti replied breathless.

"I was, but I forgot my phone so I came back to get it," he replied in a sensual manner.

Ashanti noticed the way that he was staring at her body and got wet.

"Don't start nothing. You know Seth waiting on you," Shanti told him.

"Seth can wait… ain't no way I can look at all this and leave right back out," Ahmad answered as he made his way to Ashanti and ripped off his clothes in the process.

When Ahmad stepped inside of the shower with her, Ashanti giggled when he picked her up. Ashanti moaned as he squeezed her tight and sucked on her neck. Her juices began to mix with the water and flowed freely. Ahmad lifted her higher and gave her breasts the attention they were screaming for. Ashanti let her head fall to the side and the water really hit her hair. She was glad that she had taken her bundles out and knew that she would have to settle for a bun for the night. Ashanti felt Ahmad shift a little, and then lifted her higher before he entered her sweetness.

"Ahhhh," they both moaned in unison as he slowly inserted himself into her wetness. That was their first shower session and Ashanti enjoyed every minute of it. Ahmad continued to stroke her all while placing kisses all over her upper body. When she felt herself getting ready to cum, she squeezed her pelvic muscles tight and tried to hold it in, but Ahmad wasn't having it. They had been playing a little game to see who could hold out the longest and Ashanti lost every time. Her juices flowed down her legs, and moments later, Ahmad came inside of her. Now that they were highly satiated, they both dropped to the floor and laughed.

"That shit was good as hell. I been waiting on the moment I walked in and caught you getting in the shower," he guffawed.

"I'm glad you forgot your phone," Shanti happily told him.

They both finally got up after a few minutes and showered together. Ahmad washed Ashanti first and then she returned the favor. When she looked down at his dick and saw it growing again, she smiled, but told him that she would let him make it for the moment.

After Ahmad left, Ashanti applied lotion to her body and then got dressed. She looked at the time and noticed that it was already 9:30, so she hurried her pace. She told Kya that she would pick her up at that time because Kya had a history of being slow, and the original leave time was set to 10:00. As soon as Ashanti put her earrings on and sprayed on some Gucci Guilty, the doorbell rang. Aaliyah was always prompt so she expected her right at that moment. Ashanti admired herself in her full length body mirror and headed to open the door.

"Heeyyyy… look at you," Shanti exclaimed when she opened the door and saw her friend looking all cute in black and white jumpsuit.

Aaliyah struck a pose and then twirled around. Both girls stared laughing as Liyah pulled out her phone and snapped pictures for Snap Chat. They chatted for a few more minutes and then headed out of the door. Ashanti hit the unlock button on her keyless entry vehicle and then they hopped inside.

"Why you going this way?" Liyah asked, full of curiosity.

"Oh yeah… I meant to text you and tell you I invited Kya. She needs to get out of the house," Shanti replied.

"Okay… cool. It'll probably do her some good," Liyah responded.

Ten minutes later, Ashanti turned into Forest Creek where Kya had recently moved to. She stayed with her mom when she first got out of the hospital, but let Ashanti know the last time they talked that she had moved. Ashanti understood her wanting to remain independent and get back to her normal self. After Ashanti pulled out her phone and called Kya, she walked out of the door a couple of minutes later.

Ashanti maneuvered through the side streets until she reached highway 82 and made her way towards West Point. She was happy to see Liyah and Kya getting along so well. Ashanti thanked God for a friend like Aaliyah because she was truly a gift and calm to her frequent storms. Ashanti turned the radio up, and they all sang and talked for the twenty-five minute drive until their destination was reached. The parking lot was pretty packed, and it wasn't even eleven o'clock; Ashanti was glad they left at the time they did.

After Ashanti paid for everyone to enter *Sopranos*, they walked in and observed that the place was indeed nice and laid back. They found an empty booth and sat down. All eyes were on the trio as they made their way through the place.

"Y'all drinking?" Liyah questioned after they sat down.

"I might get one drink since I'm driving, but y'all go ahead and turn up. I heard they don't check ID here anyway," Shanti noted.

"I haven't had a drink in… shit… I can't even remember, but I do need one. You wanna go grab one?" Kya said and turned towards Liyah.

"Sure," she replied and they got up. Ashanti told them to grab her an Amaretto Sour while she remained seated to secure their seats.

An hour later, the girls were up dancing and enjoying themselves as they listened to the DJ switch the music from old school to R&B to blues then back and forth.

"Damn… I gotta pee," Ashanti informed them right before they went and sat back down.

"I'll be right back," she continued and left.

Ashanti pulled her phone out as she made her way to the bathroom and sent Ahmad a selfie with her tongue sticking out and told him that she missed him. When she walked into the bathroom, she heard two girls talking from inside of separate stalls, but she didn't pay them any mind until something peaked her interest, and one of the voices started to sound familiar.

"You a damn fool… one minute you walking around pregnant and the next, your stomach flat as a wash board," one of the girls stated and laughed.

"Bitch, you know how it goes… I'm sure I won't see anyone here that knows me. College kids don't come here, and I need a quick come up for the night," the other girl replied.

After that last comment was made, Ashanti was sure that it was the bitch Sabrina behind one of those stalls, and she couldn't wait for her to come out. The bathroom door burst opened, and Kya and Aaliyah came in laughing and talking. They both noticed the scowl on Ashanti's face and simultaneously asked her what was wrong. Before she could respond, Sabrina exited the stall, and Ashanti locked eyes with her. No words were spoken as Ashanti walked up to Sabrina and punched her right in the face. As Sabrina fell backwards, Ashanti jumped down on her and commenced to beating the fuck out of her while talking shit. Her friend exited the stall after she heard all of the commotion. When she tried to hit Ashanti, Kya gave her a blow that sent her ass stumbling backwards and then proceeded to kick her ass. Ashanti felt someone pulling her away, and knew that it was Aaliyah when she heard her voice. Just as Ashanti finally stopped tagging Sabrina's trifling ass, she observed Liyah getting in a couple of kicks while cussing her out.

Interestingly enough, no one else entered the bathroom as the fight took place. Ashanti, Kya, and Aaliyah used the bathroom, washed their hands, checked themselves out in the mirror and exited the restroom like nothing had happened. The bathroom was located all the way in the back and with the music blasting, no one heard a thing. They decided to go ahead and leave just in case anyone connected them with anything. Once they got into the truck, Ashanti disclosed everything she overheard Sabrina discussed with amusement, and they all agreed she got what she deserved.

Chapter Twenty-Five

Ahmad smiled as he held his phone in his hand and looked down at the picture Ashanti had just sent him. Even though he had just taken advantage of her in the shower a little while before, his dick began rocking up as he gazed at her luscious, pretty lips.

"Damn man... is you gon' play or what?" Seth kidded.

"Nigga, you ought to be tired of getting yo ass kicked," Ahmad replied and laughed.

They had been drinking, eating pizza, playing the game and talking shit for the past couple of hours. Fall Break couldn't have come at a better time for any of them. Even though it was October, it was still warm outside, one of the perks of Mississippi weather.

Ahmad's phone rang as soon as he put it down. He picked it up and detected that it was a number that he didn't recognize. Since it was a local number, he went ahead and answered it because it could have been anybody from the basketball team in need.

"Hello," Ahmad answered with caution.

"Is this Ahmad Jones? I got your number from..." the caller said but Ahmad cut her off.

"Yes it is... who is this?" he replied with some annoyance in his voice.

"I work at Oktibbeha County Hospital, and I'm calling to inform you that your brother is here but is being airlifted to North Mississippi Medical Center in Tupelo," the lady stated.

"Wait... what? What happened?" Ahmad inquired as he got up. He noticed Seth looking at him as he also got up and grabbed his car keys.

Ahmad listened to everything the lady on the phone said as he made his way outside. Things were finally looking up, especially his relationship with his brother and then they were hit with something new. He hopped into the passenger seat of Seth's car and when he hung up, he explained everything to him as they headed towards Tupelo. Ahmad couldn't believe the turn of events as he rode in silence. Death was something that he knew was inevitable, but after recently losing his mom, he just didn't want to lose anyone else close to him. The dynamics of his relationship with his brother had changed drastically, and he knew that it would only get better in time. He said a silent prayer that God would give him another chance so that Kentay could be there for his kids.

It wasn't until Seth was near the Aberdeen exit when he spoke and broke the silence.

"You may wanna call your dad bruh," he told Ahmad.

"Damn... see I ain't cut out for this shit. I ain't thought about calling no damn body," Ahmad replied and picked his phone up out of his lap. It was after midnight so he knew his dad was more than likely sleep by now. He didn't want to wake him up since Kendra was still living with him, but there wasn't much of a choice in his eyes so he placed the call anyway.

"What's going on son?" Dennis sleepily asked after the third or fourth ring.

"Dad... it's Kentay. I don't know all of the details yet, but we are headed to Tupelo where he has been airlifted. I know you have Kendra, so I can call and update you when I get there," Ahmad replied.

"I think the lady said something about a gunshot wound," Ahmad blurted.

"Got dammit!" Dennis spat.

"What in the... Jesus. Let me see if the neighbor can... never mind. We'll be on our way soon," Dennis told his son and hung up before he could respond.

"Damn... I gotta call Shanti... wait, am I supposed to call her? Yeah, I know she cares about his well-being, even after all the shit he put her through," Ahmad stated more so to himself than to Seth.

He called her, but she didn't answer her phone, so Ahmad sent her a brief text letting her know that he was headed to Tupelo for an emergency. As soon as he put his phone back down, it rang.

"Hey babe... I couldn't answer your call because I ran a stop sign here in West Point and Officer Jackson pulled me over. He only gave me a warning though," Shanti said from the other end.

"Did you read my text?" he asked her.

"No... I just called back. Is something wrong?" she quickly inquired.

"Me and Seth headed to Tupelo. Kentay got shot, and he's being airlifted to the hospital there... I don't really know all of the details yet. We should be there in about twenty more minutes," Ahmad remarked.

"Damn… you want me to come there?" Shanti asked, not sure of what to do.

"It's up to you. I think dad is on the way already. So yeah, if you come, you can get Kendra at least," he gravely responded. Ahmad heard Ashanti briefly repeating what he told her to Aaliyah, and then they hung up with each other. He thought about calling her back and telling her not to come since she was going to see her dad the next day, but he knew that she was going to come and be with him anyway, so he left well enough alone.

A little while longer, Seth turned into North Mississippi Medical Center and parked in the first spot that he saw. Ahmad hopped out first and Seth was right behind him. When they walked in, the lady behind the desk must have recognized Ahmad because she started smiling from ear to ear. Ahmad was normally calm and used to the attention, but this time he was a bit aggravated due to the circumstances, so he cut straight to the point.

"I'm here to check on my brother," he spoke with urgency in his voice.

"Hello Mr. Jones. What's your brother's name?" the receptionist inquired.

"Yo Ahmad… hey. I'm Dub. Tay's partna. I had them write your name down. They ain't came out and said shit yet," Slick stated with frustration. Ahmad noticed the way that Slick cut his eyes at the receptionist, and he figured that the girl hadn't been much help to him.

"Let me see what I can find out. I think he's in surgery," the girl told them.

Ahmad, Seth, and Slick walked away from the desk and started talking. Slick told them what happened, but Ahmad was sure it was the simplified version, but he didn't care. He figured the less that he knew the better. After a few minutes of standing, they all finally went and sat in some chairs that were close to the window. A little over an hour later, Ahmad looked up and saw the girl walking towards them, but he couldn't read the expression on her face. He knew that it wasn't one of cheer like she presented when they first made it.

"I'm sorry to tell you this, but…" she said and Ahmad got up and hit the wall and then left. He didn't want to hear her next words.

Chapter Twenty-Six

"This is 'bout to be awkward as hell for you, ain't it?" Liyah said from the passenger seat.

"What?" Shanti asked her.

"Kentay being shot? Ahmad there. Who do you comfort? Even I'm stuck on this," Liyah replied and Ashanti saw her put her hand on her chin as if she was in deep thought.

"Girl... I'll be good. I'm so over Tay and my baby knows it, but I don't want anything bad to happen to him. He's really been a better person now that his kids are in his life," Shanti retorted.

"Shanti, you really do have a heart of gold... I'll never be able to thank you enough for forgiving me and giving me another chance," Kya cosigned.

"We all make mistakes Kya, myself included. We're good," Ashanti assured her and smiled.

"Are you okay though? I don't know how close you and Kentay got, but I know how he is," Shanti continued.

"Umm... I think it would be awkward talking about that with you," Kya nervously stated. There was a moment of silence and then all of the girls burst out laughing.

"I didn't want sex details... I just didn't know how long y'all... you know... and if your feelings ran deep," Ashanti said after they all stopped laughing.

"I care about him, but out of respect for you... I won't sleep with him again. I really don't think it would have ever happened outside of prison," Kya confessed.

"I'm happy y'all made up too though. Kya, she was missing you even though her stubborn ass may never admit it," Liyah chimed in.

"I'm supposed to go and see my dad tomorrow... I might just wait until the Sunday visit though. Depends on how long we stay up here," Shanti remarked.

"I need to get back down there too," Kya murmured.

"You can go wit' me," Shanti told her.

"I just don't know if I'm strong enough to face that place right now, but I do want to see him," Kya admitted.

"Damn... I'm sorry. It slipped my mind. Whenever you're ready, we can go together. I'm just so happy to have him back, even though it's partially," Shanti replied.

"Therapy is really helping me. I'll be sure to let you know. And, I'm glad that all of the secrets are out," Kya responded semi-elated.

All of a sudden, an eerie feeling shivered over Ashanti, but she fought to ignore it. They talked for the rest of the ride there, and it was almost two o'clock in the morning by the time they made it. Ashanti saw Ahmad standing near the entrance, so she parked in the first spot that she saw, and it was very close to the front. She didn't care that it was reserved for handicap, all she had on her mind was reaching Ahmad because he appeared to be upset to her. Ashanti ran towards him, and when their eyes locked, she knew something was terribly wrong.

"What's wrong babe?" she asked in a panic as soon as she reached him.

Instead of replying, Ahmad fell into her arms, and she hugged him tight. She could feel him fighting back tears as his chest heaved up and down.

"I got you baby... I got you," was all Ashanti could manage to say.

"Aye Mad... it wasn't Kentay that died," Seth came running out of the door yelling.

"What?" Ahmad turned around and asked bewildered.

"How 'bout there's a guy named Kenta without the *y* here but his last name is Miller. That girl wasn't paying much attention when I asked," another dude standing behind Seth stated. He looked familiar to Ashanti, but she couldn't place him.

"Hey Shanti... I'm Dub," he said when he saw the look on her face.

"Oh... that's right. Hey Dub. So Kentay is fine?" she sincerely queried.

"Now that part we still don't know... but ol' girl told us that he died, but it was someone else," he explained as he shrugged his shoulders and shook his head.

"He's gon' be okay," Ashanti told Ahmad as she rubbed his back. She could tell that he was a little relieved but still had some doubts. She tried her best to comfort him, but the nagging feeling that she had in the pit of her stomach just wouldn't go away. She looked up and saw that Aaliyah and Seth were joined at the hip, while Kya just stood there in a trance.

"What's wrong?" Ashanti leaned over and whispered.

"I don't know... something just feels off, but I don't know what it is," Kya told her.

"I been having a weird feeling too, but I just kept it to myself," Shanti conferred.

"Everything is gonna be okay though," she continued and smiled.

"Let's go back inside so we won't miss any updates," Liyah said out loud and everyone agreed.

Fifteen minutes after they had been sitting in the waiting area, a doctor walked out and asked for the Mill's family. Ahmad stood up and made his way over to the doctor.

"Hello... I'm Dr. Jacobs and I came out here to give you all an update. We performed the first surgery to the neck area, and it was successful. However, the second one is about to begin. I wanted to notify you all that you may not hear back from anyone for the next four to five hours due to the difficulty of the surgery. Unfortunately, one of the bullets is lodged right here," the doctor said as he pointed at his heart, causing everyone to gasp loudly.

"We are hopeful that we will successfully be able to remove it, but it won't be an easy task. You guys remain prayerful, and I will send a nurse out here if I can to update you all as much as possible," Dr. Jacobs deliberated and then walked away.

"This 'bout to be one long ass night. Let me see where dad is," Ahmad said and then pulled out his phone.

"I guess I can go move my truck and grab my phone," Shanti said and stood up.

"I'll walk out with you," Kya told her and stood up as well.

They walked outside and talked about how they felt like everything was going to be okay with Kentay. Ashanti didn't want Ahmad to have to deal with losing his brother since he had conveyed to her about how much he wanted their relationship to grow. Ashanti and Kya hopped in the truck and viewed a parking space not too far from where they were parked. Ashanti maneuvered into the space and then she picked up her phone. She saw a few missed calls, but before she clicked on the phone icon to see who they were from, her phone rang again. It was her mom and she wondered what she was doing up so late. Ashanti answered and all she heard was her mom crying and screaming. Once she heard a few chopped up words and pieced them together, Ashanti lost it.

"NOOOOOO! NOOOOO! NOOOOOOO!!" she screamed over and over and over.

Chapter Twenty-Seven

"Aye... I know it ain't been all that smooth between us, but I really wanna squash the beef and move forward," Big Al heard someone say behind him. He turned around and noticed that it was one of the cats who had always fully hated and envied him.

"I don't have a beef to squash. Everything is everything on my end," he casually replied.

"Let's pray together then," the guy said.

Those words caught Big Al off guard. Even though he was one not to be fucked with, everyone knew that he was big on prayer. He would feel like a hypocrite if he turned down the opportunity to pray with anyone, especially when they asked, so he agreed and had prayer with the guy. It was like a chain reaction because before he knew it, just about everyone had joined in on that prayer. Earlier that day, Big Al had been feeling like something was about to go wrong, but after the prayer, he went to his cell and shrugged it off. After he read a few scriptures, wrote letters to his daughters, and prayed again, he went to sleep.

The next day, Big Al got up and started his day the same as he normally did, except he doubled his push-ups. It seemed as if the day was dragging by, but on a rare occasion, everyone seemed to be getting along. Big Al played a few games of chess with some of the youngsters and schooled them throughout. On any other day, Big Al would skip dinner on Friday's, but he decided to eat in the cafeteria and then take his shower. He chowed down on the hamburger steak, mashed potatoes, green beans, and corn bread.

After Big Al finished eating, he made his way towards the showers. On his way in, the same dude that he had the so called truce with was on his way out. They spoke and Big Al kept it moving. As soon as he removed all of his clothing and stepped under the water, Big Al heard some commotion at the door.

"I heard about y'all lil plan... it ain't going down... yo, Big Al—" he heard the youngster who he had been playing chess with earlier say. His sentence ended abruptly, and Big Al knew something was wrong. As soon as he turned around, he caught a glimpse of the guy as he fell to the floor with blood gushing out of his neck. A few seconds later, he felt a sharp pain in his back that caused him to double over in pain.

"You thought a lil prayer meant something to me... that didn't mean shit," Big Al heard before he felt stabs, punches, kicks, and cuts all over his body. He tried his best to fight back, but he was tremendously outnumbered. A few minutes later, Big Al felt himself losing consciousness. He sensed that it was the end for him. Big Al thought about how he underestimated the guy after he had pounded him to a bloody pulp for violating his daughter. If he could do it all over again, Big Al told himself that he wouldn't change a thing. He had a long run in and outside of prison, and he had no regrets. Big Al whispered a few words before he took his last breath.

"Lord... please forgive me for my sins and keep my family safe!"

***

Tina pranced around the kitchen singing and dancing as she prepared one of her husband's favorite meals. She was so thankful that the grudge she had been carrying for him was gone and was even more elated that he had so many inside and outside connections that allowed them to do things that the other inmates could only dream about. She intended to get up bright and early the next morning to go visit him, carrying enough food with her to last Big Al for a few days.

Tina fixed herself a plate, poured a glass of Roscato, and sat down in front of the TV to watch the recording of *Scandal* from the night before. She loved how Shonda Rhimes displayed current events into the show, and if people paid closer attention, they would notice the underlying messages. Tina put a piece of roast in her mouth and smiled at its tenderness. She knew that her husband was going to love it and his mouth would water just from the scent. After she finished eating, Tina traveled to her bedroom, walked into her en suite, and ran a steaming hot bubble bath. Once the tub was filled to her satisfaction, she poured another glass of wine and then stepped in, sat down, and exhaled.

After Tina's body was relaxed, she washed off and got out of the tub. She dried her body with her one of her favorite cream colored plush towels and then caressed her body with a new body butter she had recently purchased. When her body hit those silk sheets, she was out within minutes after fantasizing about the next day. The house phone rang and jarred Tina out of her peaceful sleep. When she looked at the clock on her nightstand, she wondered who in the hell could be calling her at almost midnight.

"Hello," she sleepily answered.

"I'm so sorry Tina," was all the voice said and she knew who it was right away. She could tell that Joe had been crying.

"What's wrong Joe? What happened?" Tina sat up and asked the security guard who had been nothing short of a blessing to her.

"They caught him off guard and he didn't make it," Joe managed to tell her.

Tears streamed down Tina's face as she listened to Joe run the story down to her. All kinds of emotions ran through her veins. She couldn't believe what she was hearing, but she knew that Joe was always straightforward and honest. When Tina finally hung up the phone, she really lost it. She thought about all of the years that she wasted hating him, only for Big Al to die a few short months after they had reunited and had gotten back on track.

"Whyyyyyy? Whhhyyyyy? Whhhyyyy?" Tina screamed over and over and over again. It was good that she didn't have neighbors close enough to hear her or they would have been knocking on her door in a panic. Tina knew that she needed to call her daughter to deliver the sad news, but she dreaded it wholeheartedly.

A little over an hour later, Tina finally gathered her nerves and picked up the phone to call Shanti. She dialed Ashanti a few times, but she didn't answer. She knew Ashanti was a light sleeper and always heard her phone, so she called again. This time, she answered. When Tina heard her daughter's voice, she started crying uncontrollably again. She could barely get her words out, but when she heard Ashanti screaming through the phone, Tina realized that her baby discerned her words and understood that she just lost her father.

Chapter Twenty-Eight

"Baby, I gotta run and go see my partna. I don't know what all happened, but you're free to come with me or I can take you by my crib," Slick said as soon as they hopped into his truck. Dub had been updating him, but his phone died so Slick hadn't heard back from him in over an hour. He was eager to get to Tupelo, but he didn't want to force Amanda to have to go, and it would only take about fifteen minutes to run her to his place.

"I'm kinda tired, so if you don't mind, will you just take me to your place so I can get a little rest?" Amanda pleaded.

"That's cool... I need you resting with my seed anyway," he told her.

The fake smile that she just gave him and the feeling in his gut was nagging at Slick. After landing back home from their abrupt vacation, Slick observed the unsettling mood change in Amanda's attitude and body language. Something was very off with Amanda, and he couldn't quite put his finger on it. As he drove towards his place, he remained silent as troubling thoughts ran rapid through his mind.

"If you don't want this baby, I won't force you to have it. Will I be upset? Of course, that's my first seed, but I know I can't force you to do anything you don't want to. That will only cause you to resent me and the baby later," Slick petitioned when he turned into his place. He needed to see where Amanda's head was at.

"No baby... I'm happy. I'm just kinda scared. This is all new to me," she told him. As clear as day, the unenthusiastic tone in her voice alerted him that her quick response was some rehearsed bullshit.

"We gon' be alright. You just gotta trust me. You trust me right?" he asked her.

"Of course I do," she replied, a little too hasty for his taste.

"Good... you come on in here and get some rest. I'll be back before you know it," Slick instructed.

As he ushered Amanda inside his place, Slick had a bad feeling to wash over him. Slick led Amanda to his room and gave her a kiss before he headed back out. Before he left, he made sure that his alarm was secure and double checked the audio on his surveillance. Slick's instincts told him to stay nearby, so he said a prayer that his boy would be fine and planned on doing just that. In the past, when he listened to his gut feeling like the one he was experiencing at the moment, it was always proved right. The liquor stores were closed, and he was out of Hennessey and needed a shot badly. Slick decided to head out to the trap house in Black Jack to grab a few items. He felt conflicted because he really did love Amanda. Deep down, he always felt like something was off, but he just didn't know exactly what. His mind convinced him that he needed to find out soon and very soon.

When Slick made it to his destination in Black Jack, he grabbed his phone and headed inside. First thing first, he grabbed some Pineapple Ciroc from their stash and poured himself a drink. After he threw back a double shot, Slick sat down on the couch and clicked on the ADT app for his security system. Once the app was up and running, Slicked watched as Amanda paced his bedroom floor and her body language indicated that she was upset. Her phone rang, causing her to practically jump out of her skin to answer it.

"I can't do this shit no more," he heard Amanda declare when he turned the audio volume up. Slick wished that he could hear who was on the other end of the phone, but to his disadvantage, he was only able to hear one side of the conversation. After she made that statement, she took the phone away from her ear, looked at it like she was either sending a text message or ignoring a call, and then put it back to her ear.

"You told me that you were gonna get rid of Kya while she was in the hospital. Now, her ass is out of the hospital and living her life like her shit don't stink. Do you even care that she killed Blow?" Amanda vented.

"I hear what you saying, but this shit has been going on for far too long; and now, I know Slick is feeling some type of way. He thinks I'm pregnant so that might buy me a little more time, but I'm fuckin' tired of this shit. This whole shitty plan of yours has been over. I know he wants Kya anyway. You remember he fucked her right before I followed him to the IHOP," Amanda screamed.

As Slick listened to her sole confession, he didn't even allow himself to become too upset. He blamed himself for not doing his homework thoroughly before he completely let her into his life. This predicament was all on him, so he had to be the one to fix it. Slick finished off the bottle of liquor and began to strategically formulate a plan in his head. He listened to Amanda rigorously as she carried on her conversation and felt like a complete fool. Him and Kya were pawns from the very beginning, and he contended that not only was Amanda related to the Blow character, but she also had something to do with the shooting that took place in Memphis that time.

He had heard enough, so he exited the surveillance app and got up to leave. Even though he blamed himself, Slick found himself becoming angrier as he prepared to make his exit. Slick didn't have a solid plan just yet, but one thing was for sure, Amanda had to be dealt with immediately. After a few more minutes, Slick locked up the place, slid into his truck, and hit the road to head back home. Less than fifteen minutes later, he pulled up at his place and parked. Slick typed up a long text and hit send before he changed his mind.

He sat in the truck for about five more minutes before finally venturing out of it. Slick didn't know if he would receive a quick reply to the text or not, but he knew it would come eventually. At least, he hoped it would. Slick walked into his apartment and proceeded straight to his bedroom. Amanda tried to hop in the bed, but it was pointless because he saw her.

"Why you back so quickly? What's wrong?" she asked when he made his way over to the side of the bed that she occupied.

"I needed to come back and take care of something. I figured you would be sleeping by now," Slick calmly replied. He walked over to her and rubbed her chin, and Amanda flinched a little.

"What's wrong? Yo heart beating fast as fuck," he remarked as he placed his hand on her chest.

"I.I.I… I felt a little sick. I been up since you left," Amanda stuttered.

"Why you so jumpy though?" he quizzically inquired.

"Noth… no reason. You kinda scared me when you came in though," Amanda replied.

"Amanda… Amanda… Amanda… we not gon' prolong this shit. Just tell me why you did it… matter fact… don't even answer that," he said as he sat down beside her on the bed.

"What are yo—?" she started saying, however Slick threw up his right hand to silence her, cutting off her words immediately.

"Don't even try it… don't fucking sit here and lie to me in my face," Slick seethed, trying to keep his wayward emotions at bay.

141

"Are you really pregnant?" Slick wanted to know after reflecting on her persistence of not being pregnant.

"No! I'm not," she admitted, letting out a loud sigh of relief. "And before you even ask, I planned the whole thing. I stole a pregnancy test from a friend, who just found out she was pregnant. When we stopped and got the test in Puerto Rico, I put the store bag in my purse and managed to open the box without your knowledge, and slipped her test in the box. You made it easy for me when we got back to the room. You went out on the balcony while I went into the bathroom to take the test. And voilà, I'm pregnant," she explained. He could tell by the expression on her face that she felt like if she was honest at this point, it would save her life, but the damage had already been done.

"Wow... Fuck man! I didn't believe I was that gullible, but you proved me wrong. So, how was you going to... never mind. It's a moot point anyways. I'll give you credit though, you played the hell out of your part, so damn convincing," he said with a lot of indifference and loathing.

"I'm sorry," Amanda muttered as she burst out crying.

"I did love you... I did, but it's my fault that I looked over the signs of the conniving bitch that you were," Slick grunted and grabbed Amanda around the neck. He didn't want a blood bath with her, but he needed her gone. He tightened the grip on her neck, and choked the gruesome life out of Amanda until she took her last breath. Slick was frustrated as hell, even hurt from the betrayal of it all. But at the end of the day, that was just another hard and painful lesson that he had to learn. *Never. Again,* he vowed to himself.

Chapter Twenty-Nine

For the past week, everything evolved in slow motion for Ashanti. Ahmad had been by her side every step of the way. Instead of being angry and upset about what had happened, she tried to look at things from a different angle. Ashanti found herself being strong for Kya because she blamed herself for their dad's death. She knew that something else was going on with Kya when she received a text from her the night before asking Ashanti to meet her at *Stagger Inn*. They had all been together at the wake, and everyone agreed to get some rest before the funeral the next day, but things never went according to plan in their lives.

When Ashanti arrived at the location, she walked in and linked eyes with Kya and Slick sitting at a table in the back, making her way over to them. She didn't tell Kya that Ahmad would be with her because she knew it didn't matter, but she was very surprised to see Slick. She looked around wondering if Kentay was about to pop up as well. He had been discharged from the hospital on Monday, and everything was going fine with him. Surgery for him was a success, and he was in recovery when everyone made their way back in the hospital after receiving the news about Big Al.

"Hey y'all... did y'all finally stop playing games and make this official?" Ashanti quizzically inquired when she sat down.

"Slick don't want me. I'm damaged goods," Kya mumbled. "But that ain't why I called you," Kya hurriedly continued. Ashanti saw Slick lean over and whisper something in Kya's ear, and she could tell that she was holding back a smile.

"Anyways... Slick walked in right after I texted you. My intentions were to vent to you, and the situation does involve him so it might be a little awkward," Kya stated.

"You wanna go sit at the bar for a minute while they talk?" Ahmad asked Slick and he agreed to the suggestion. They both got up and walked away at the same time.

"What's going on?" Shanti asked right away.

"It seems like shit just always happens back to back to back," Kya said and sighed heavily with irritation.

"Tell me about it... we gonna get through it all though," Shanti said in an attempt to comfort her sister.

"It's about Amanda... I really thought she was my friend, but I guess she was just on some crazy mission," Kya said and shook her head.

Ashanti listened attentively as Kya repeated the story that she said Slick had given her. She listened very carefully as Kya read a text message that she received from Slick and then talked about everything that had been going on. Ashanti could tell that Kya was extremely hurt by this girl's action. She watched Kya fight back tears as she discussed how Amanda was there for her every single time she needed her and as she expressed her concerns about who else might be looking for her.

"I guess all of this shit is just karma," Kya said after she finally finished talking.

"Everybody goes through shit in their lives. Some more than others, but that's just how it goes. You're not gonna beat yourself up over what this chick did. You're gonna keep moving forward. WE are gonna keep moving forward. Slick will handle everything. You know that," Ashanti adamantly stated while she wrapped her arms around her sister's shoulders to comfort her.

"Besides... all of this might have happened so you two can finally be together openly. Who knows? You're getting back in school in January. You're already working. Everything is looking up for you, and you will get your fresh start," Shanti continued to encourage Kya.

"I'm not looking for a man right now Shanti," Kya replied and took a sip of her Strawberry Margarita.

"You don't have to be looking. That man has been in your face for years, and you used him like a piece of meat. It's clear that he cares for you. Don't focus on the past, move forward, sis," Ashanti sincerely stated. Ashanti turned around and motioned for Ahmad to come back and join them an hour later. He walked back over with Slick and they all sat there and talked for another hour or so. Ashanti was dreading the next day, but about midnight, the foursome finally parted ways so that they all could prepare to say their final goodbyes to Big Al.

The next morning, Ashanti woke up around eight o'clock, but she didn't move. Her body was numb. The funeral was set for noon at First Unity in Weir. Ashanti hadn't been to her home church in a while, but her mom attended faithfully and handled every detail for the service. They didn't want to do a family car or anything like that, but they all agreed to meet up at her mom's no later than 11:30. An hour had passed before Ashanti knew it and Ahmad began prompting her to get up.

"Come on babe. We gotta get moving," he told her and pulled her up.

"I've been good all this week, but I'm not sure I can do this today," Ashanti replied barely above a whisper.

"I got you baby. I ain't gon' lie and say it'll be easy, but I'll be with you every step of the way. We will get through this together," Ahmad replied and pulled Ashanti in for a bear hug.

For the first time since she received that dreadful call from her mom telling her that her dad died, Ashanti cried. She had been willing herself to be strong like people had advised her to be, but at the moment, she didn't want to be strong. She wanted to just be weak, if only for the moment.

"I admire you for being so strong, love, but don't you drive yourself crazy thinking you aren't supposed to show any emotions and shit. We all human," Ahmad soothed as she continued to cry.

An hour later, Ashanti and Ahmad were both dressed and ready to head out. Since navy blue was Big Al's favorite color, they all decided to wear that color in memory of him. Ahmad asked her if she wanted to grab something to eat before they left out of Starkville, but she declined. The ride to Weir was quiet. Traffic was light, so Ahmad made it to Tina's house in about thirty minutes. After sitting in the car for a few minutes, Ashanti looked up and saw her mom and Kya standing at the front door talking. Ashanti knew that her mom had been purposely keeping herself busy as a distraction. Judging by the look on Tina's face, she recognized that her mom was near her breaking point.

Ashanti and Ahmad finally exited the vehicle and went inside of the house. The TV was on *Centric* and reruns of *Martin* were playing in the background. Everyone in the house was very quiet as they sat in the living room, just waiting for the time to pass by. Ashanti got up, went into the kitchen, and grabbed a knife when she saw the fresh caramel cake on the counter. After she ate a slice and drank a glass of milk, she glanced at the clock on the microwave and noticed that it was already 11:30. Her mom told everyone that they would be heading to the church at a quarter till twelve, so they could leave and head to the church. It was located right over the hill from Tina's house and was less than sixty seconds away.

"Come on! Let's go everyone!" Tina walked through the house saying. When Ashanti walked outside, the yard was full. She saw Kentay's truck, and someone was inside with him, but she couldn't tell who. When she looked to the left, Slick was leading Kya to his car. Aaliyah and Seth were right in front of her, and Ahmad was between her and her mom. Everyone else fell in place and headed to their cars.

When they made it up the hill, cars were everywhere. Ashanti's stomach started to turn as realization stunned her that she was really about to say goodbye to her dad. She sat on the backseat and glanced over at her mom, who had her sunglasses on. Ashanti instantly noticed the tears running down her left cheek. She was just ready to get the funeral and cemetery services over with. As soon as Ahmad stopped in front of the church, Ashanti jumped out of the vehicle and ran to the bathroom. She felt sick to her stomach. There wasn't much on her stomach, but all of it came up and then she dry heaved for about two minutes. She felt a gentle hand on her back and heard her mother's voice in the distance.

"You okay babe?" Ahmad asked, not caring that he had entered the women's bathroom.

"Yeah, I'm fine. I don't know what came over me," Shanti replied, still feeling the remnants of her sudden bout of illness.

"It's my grandson that made her throw up," Tina chimed in as a way to deflect from the obvious sadness they were feeling and the real reason that they were attending church that day.

"Huh… I'm not pregnant mom," Ashanti replied as she headed over to the sink to wash her mouth out. She had thrown up a few days ago, but she knew she wasn't pregnant. Ashanti told herself that missing one pill shouldn't hurt a thing.

"Baby, can you get my purse please? I have a travel pack in it with a toothbrush and stuff in it," Shanti asked.

"Sure. I'll be right back," he told her.

Ashanti stared at her mom after she threw a paper towel in the garbage.

"I'm not pregnant mom," she said with as much fervent she could muster.

"You'll see," her mom said and walked up to her and hugged her.

Ahmad was back in record time, and Ashanti brushed her teeth, gargled with mouthwash, and was good to go. Her stomach still felt funny, but she was at a funeral, so she didn't expect it to stop any time soon. Kya walked into the bathroom moments later, and Ashanti teared up as she noticed her bloodshot red eyes. Ashanti immediately pulled her into her embrace, and they both broke down crying. Before long, Tina had finally broken down her guards, and she lost it as well. Ahmad tried his best to console all three of them, but ushers made their way into the stall and took over.

The funeral didn't start until almost 12:30, and everything was a blur to Ashanti. She remembered a few songs, some people giving acknowledgments, but the only person that was memorable to her was when Kentay got up and spoke. It was the most genuine that she had ever seen him. She figured that her dad must have really given him a hard time while he was in jail, but evidently, it helped shaped him into becoming a better person.

They made it through the funeral and the repast, and later on that evening, Tina's house was packed. There was an endless supply of food and drinks. Like after all black people's funerals, it turned into a party. Ashanti finally found her appetite and was fixing her second plate when Kentay walked into the kitchen.

"Your dad really was a good man. He gave me hell, but I know the reasoning behind it and I deserved it," he told her.

"I have someone I want you to meet before we leave," he told her before she had a chance to reply.

"Okay… and it's strange how all of this played out," Shanti responded. Kentay called someone by the name of Courtney and a female walked in.

"This is Kendall's mom and my fiancée, Courtney. Courtney, this is Ashanti, my brother's future wife," Kentay introduced the two. They both smiled and spoke and made small talk. Ahmad made his way into the kitchen and got down on one knee.

"The timing may never be what we want it to be, but I want to make the rest of this day memorable in more ways than one. I know it may not be ideal to propose to you on the day of your dad's funeral, but it just feels like the best way to end this day. He granted me his blessings and well-wishes, and I've been carrying this box around for over a month now. Our relationship didn't start out ideal. I remember when I first saw you on campus, and you didn't even know who I was. You looked at me like I was a bum asking for some change, and I knew that I had to have you. You mean the world to me baby. You are my queen, and I want to spend the rest of my life making you happy. Ashanti McNeal, will you marry me?" Ahmad passionately pleaded and opened the box.

Ashanti's eyes were full of tears as she stared at the biggest ring that she had ever laid eyes on.

"Of course I'll marry you baby!" Ashanti screamed with gusto and burst into tears. Ahmad stood up and kissed her with fervor before he picked her up and squeezed her tight to him. The room erupted into *oohs* and *ahhs* and claps and people offering their congratulations.

"You turned one of the worst days of my life into the best day of my life. I will love you forever," Ashanti sincerely told Ahmad after they finished kissing while she was still embraced in the safety of his strong hold.

Chapter Thirty

Two Months Later…

School was out for Christmas break, and Ashanti didn't plan on doing anything except working and lounging. Things would never be '*normal*' again, but she was moving forward and making the best of everything. Ashanti was lying on the couch watching *Best Man Holiday* when Ahmad walked in from practice. He walked over to her, placed a Wal-Mart bag down on the floor, and then kissed her gently. Ashanti immediately became aroused and pulled Ahmad down on her. Her sex drive had been through the roof for the past month, and she didn't know why, but Ahmad always satisfied her and left a smile on her face.

Ashanti pulled her tank top over her head and then pulled her shorts off. Since she had gotten out of the shower about twenty minutes ago, she didn't have on a bra or any panties. She became wetter as she watched Ahmad strip out of his clothes.

"How you want this dick today?" he goaded.

"Fast and rough," Ashanti devilishly replied.

As soon as those words left her mouth, Ahmad lifted both of her legs over his shoulders and dove into her tight wetness. Ashanti screamed out in pleasure and pain as he hit her spot on every single stroke. She dug her nails into his back that guaranteed to leave passion marks. Ahmad didn't seem to mind at all because he never missed a beat.

"Ohhh shit baby… dammnnn," Ashanti moaned when she felt herself about to cum.

"Let that shit go," Ahmad prompted her as he continued to stroke her, alternating from long to short at any time.

"Noooo," she screamed and tried not to climax.

"Let… that… shit… go," Ahmad commanded between pumps after he lifted her right leg up further in the air. Ashanti had no more control over her body as her juices began to flow like the Mississippi River.

"Ahhhh!" Ahmad and Ashanti screamed out in unison as he filled her up with cum.

They laid there in each other's arms for a few minutes, each with their own thoughts until Ahmad finally broke the silence.

"Grab that bag and go handle that," Ahmad demanded while he tapped her on the hips.

"Huh?" Ashanti quizzically inquired.

"Grab that bag down there and go handle that," he instructed again and then sat up so that Ashanti could move.

Ashanti reached and grabbed the bag from the floor and looked inside. When her surprised gaze met Ahmad's, all he did was point towards the back to the bathroom.

"How you—?" she started to say.

"I know you and I know your body. Just go," he cut her off and said.

Ashanti slowly got up and made her way to the bathroom. Inside of the bag were about five pregnancy tests. When her mom told her that she was pregnant the day of her dad's funeral, she just brushed her mom off like she was just crazy and wanted some grandkids of her own since Kendra had been mostly in Jackson with Kentay the past few months. Ashanti had only missed one pill and figured that shouldn't hurt. When her period didn't come on last month, she chalked it up to stress. It was due a couple of weeks ago again, and Ashanti began to worry. She thought back to her previous pregnancy and got sad. She didn't want to go down that road again, so she kept progressing forward and removed the thought of pregnancy far from her mind.

Clearly, Ahmad didn't push the possibility of pregnancy from his mind, and evidently, he knew her as well as he said. Ashanti was baffled as she stared at three of the five pregnancy tests that she had taken, with each one citing a positive result.

"This ain't a research paper, baby. What you doing?" Ahmad asked as he opened the door and walked into the bathroom with her. When he looked down at the tests and saw the results, his eyes lit up with pure joy. He scooped her up and planted kisses all over her face.

"I knew it... your mom knew it too," he exclaimed exuberantly.

"I'm scared Ahmad," Ashanti finally admitted as her eyes watered with tears.

"I know baby, but I promise you it won't be the same this time around," he told her.

"Are you really… happy? You didn't wanna wait until after we got married to have a baby?" she asked, feeling a little skeptical.

"Hell yeah I'm happy. I ain't worried about all that. Everything happens for a reason," Ahmad told her. He continued to persuade her how this pregnancy was a good thing. After truly hearing and listening to his declarations, Ashanti finally found herself smiling when she realized that he was genuinely happy. She said a prayer that things would go differently throughout her pregnancy this time around and then she rushed out of the bathroom to grab her phone and call her mom. Before she was able to hit the *call* button, the doorbell rang, and she went to open it. She was faced with blue balloons, a cake, cupcakes, and bags by everyone that she loved. Her mom was the first to walk in, followed by Dennis, Kya, Aaliyah, and Seth. Ashanti was overwhelmed with joy. She turned to look for her baby and smiled at Ahmad when she noticed him staring at her. After everything that she encountered, endured, and survived in her young life, she knew that God blessed her with the love of her life and that their baby was the ultimate gift and a testament to their love. Ahmad was her everything and not only did he complete her life, but he complimented it in every way. She was scared and wildly excited for the new beginnings that welcomed them. One thing was for sure, Ashanti couldn't wait to say "*I do*" to Ahmad so that she could spend the rest of her life loving him.

Epilogue

One Year Later...

The majestic black lava rocks running to the blue Pacific, the brilliant sunsets, the warm trade winds, and the lush foliage was all set for the private wedding ceremony at the oceanfront *Royal Kona Resort* in Hawaii. It had been exactly fourteen months since Ahmad proposed, twelve months since they found out they were having a baby, and three months since they welcomed AJ into the world, weighing seven pounds and eleven ounces. It was ironic how the timing played out, but Ashanti saw fit to get married on the date that Ahmad had proposed. He told her that he wanted to turn the worst day of her life into the best, and he had done just that.

Ashanti stared at herself in the floor length mirror and was pleased with her custom made ivory and silver vintage sheath wedding gown. Ahmad had flown Krystal MzTrecie Gibbs out to do hair and Haley Love to do makeup for the crew, and they all looked flawless. Ashanti, Kya, and Aaliyah took snapshots up until it was time for the ceremony to start.
***

"Can you believe you 'bout to be married in a few minutes and then we both about to play our first NBA game in a month, against each other," Seth grinned. Ahmad had been drafted to the Miami Heat and Seth was with the Atlanta Hawks.

"Yep... I believe it bruh. I saw all of this happening before it even took place," Ahmad replied and smiled.

"I can't thank you two enough for being here and being a part of this day," Ahmad said to Kentay and Seth.

"It's all good. I wouldn't have it any other way," Kentay replied.

"I know things between us didn't start off on the right foot, but I'm glad that we worked our way through it bruh. Marriage is gonna look good on you," Kentay continued.

"Thanks bruh, and it looks good on you. I can't believe you didn't tell us you were getting married," Ahmad said.

"Well... we just kinda decided to go ahead and do it... BOTH of us this time," Kentay said and chuckled. "When Courtney finished her last treatment, we celebrated by making our family official. If you woulda told me that my life was going to be like this a year ago, I woulda cussed you out without a second thought. But, I can honestly say that I'm loving it. We six months in and got a lifetime to go," Kentay stated.

"That's deep bruh," Ahmad said and gave Kentay a hug.

"You up next," he turned to Seth and said.

"Maannn… you know it's probably all on Liyah's mind, but we good," Seth enlightened. After the serious talks were over, they all talked shit to each other until it was time for Ahmad to marry his soul mate.

***

Ahmad, Seth, Kentay, and the pastor took their places, and the music began shortly after. As *Spend My Life With You* by Tamia and Eric Benet played, Kya and Aaliyah made their way down the aisle in their silver dresses. They were followed by Kendall pulling Kendra and AJ in a wagon. It was a beautiful sight to see. Dennis and Tina smiled at their grandkids and their smiles were contagious. Slick and Courtney were in attendance to witness the ceremony, and they were happy for the couple as well.

As Ashanti made her way down the aisle, all eyes were on her. Tina fought back tears as she admired her daughter's beauty. The water from the ocean was the only sound that could be heard, along with a few sniffles as Ashanti made her way to her husband to be. When she reached him, she couldn't stop herself from giving him a kiss.

"We haven't made it to that part of the ceremony yet," the officiator laughed and stated, which caused everyone in attendance to laugh as well. They recited their vows, performed the salt ceremony instead of lighting candles, and when the officiator made their marriage official, they kissed again, except with more passion, rigor, and longer this time.

As soon as the ceremony was over and the pictures were done, Slick walked up to Kya and got down on one knee. Before he could open the box and ask her to marry him, Kya was in tears and screaming *yes*. Ashanti and Ahmad were genuinely happy and didn't mind sharing their special day with their sister. Ashanti knew that Slick was exactly what Kya needed, and she couldn't be happier for her. Everyone enjoyed the rest of their week-long vacation before it was time to face the real world again.

The End

Note From The Author:

I really hope you all enjoyed the final installment of Pretty Lips That Thugs Love. This book by far has been the hardest for me to write. Not because of the story, but because of personal issues I had going on. I work as a therapist by day, and this past month has been really draining. I had to take breaks from writing when writing is usually my therapy. I didn't want to rush this book and just put anything out there. Some of you stayed in my inbox, but I know it was all love. I really hope that it was worth the wait. Now, it's on to the next one!! ☺

As always, I would love to have your honest feedback to help me excel in my passion. When you are done, please leave me a review on Amazon, Good Reads, and/or any of my social media, and I will reply. My Facebook, Instagram, and Twitter handles are all @authortwylat.

You may also email me at authortwylat@gmail.com

Search Twyla T's Reading Group on Facebook if you love my work and become a supporter!

Other great reads by Author Twyla T.
We Both Can't Be Bae 1-3
I'll Never Love A Dope Boy Again 1-2
My Shawty: An Original Love Story 1-3 (Pinned under TWYLA, but it's mine)
Pretty Lips That Thugs Love (1-2)

CPSIA information can be obtained
at www.ICGtesting.com
Printed in the USA
LVOW03s1719060617
537135LV00017B/325/P